ALMOST MARRIED

KYLIE GILMORE

Cover design by Sweet 'N Spicy Designs

Published by: Extra Fancy Books

ISBN-13: 978-1-942238-03-4

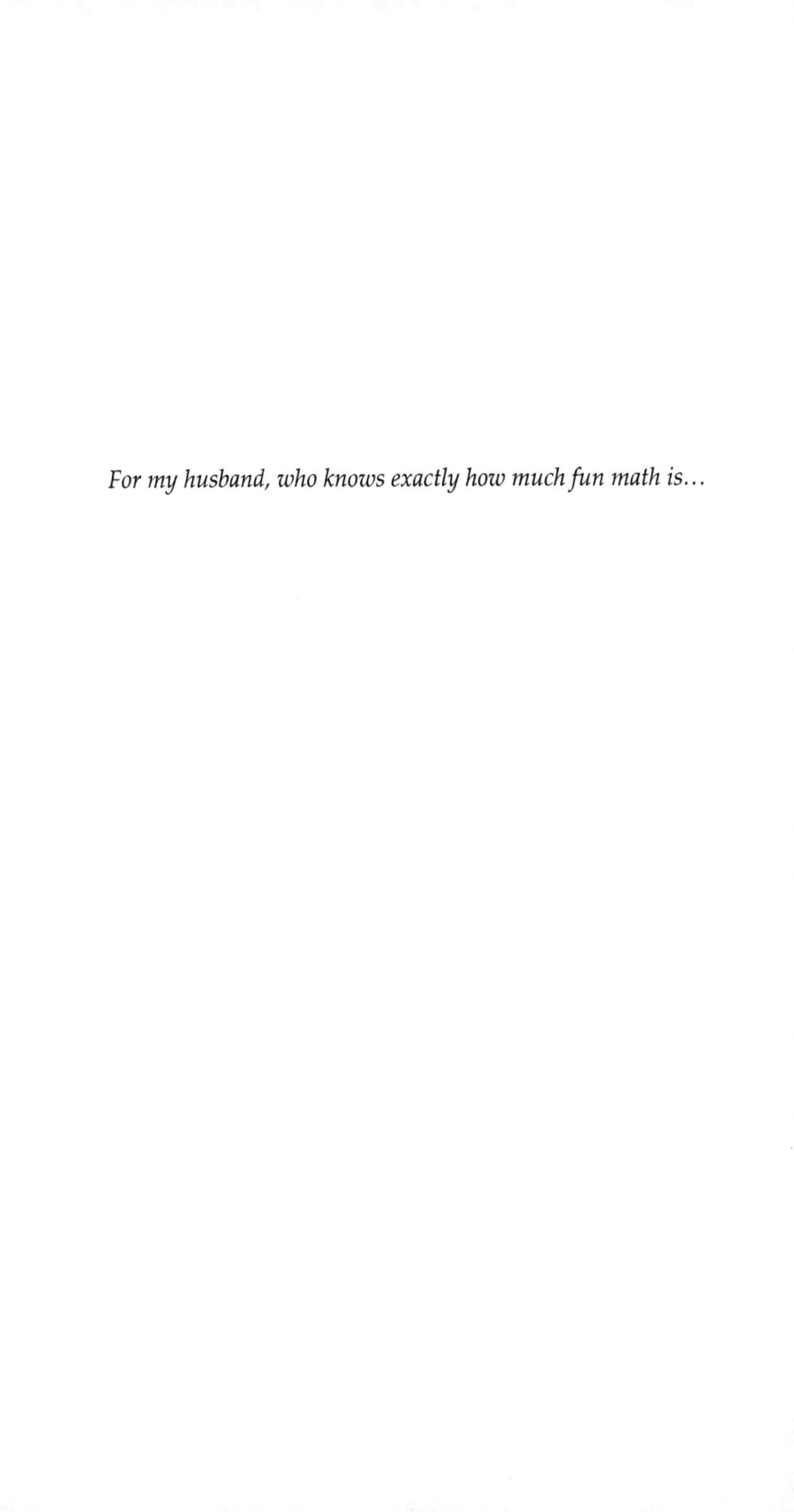

For my husband, who knows exactly how much fun math is…

1

———

Stephanie Moore's boyfriend of six weeks was a perfect gentleman. It was time to fix that.

"You could spend the night tonight," Steph whispered in Dave Olsen's ear as they slow danced at her friend Amber Lewis's (now Lewis-Furnukle) wedding reception. They were in a gorgeous mansion owned by the town of Clover Park, Connecticut, that was frequently rented out for special events.

Dave startled at her words, veering right suddenly and stomping on her foot.

"Ow!"

"Sorry!"

Steph cringed and stepped out of the danger zone. The man was a solid six foot two, and her poor toes couldn't take much more "dancing" with him.

"Could you get me more champagne?" she asked. "No, make it vodka."

"No problem," he said, pushing up his black-rimmed glasses. "Be right back." He stopped suddenly and kissed her cheek. "Sorry about all the toe crunching."

She waved that away. "No worries."

He left to get her drink. Steph took a seat with a sigh, smoothed out her lavender bridesmaid dress, and watched Amber and Bare slow dancing. No toe crunching there. They moved beautifully together. Bare whispered something in Amber's ear, and she giggled. Steph wondered what it would take to get Dave to step it up a notch in the sex department, as in, maybe they could have some. At thirty-two, Steph was way past playing hard-to-get, and Dave, at thirty, really should've taken the hint by now. Subtlety seemed to be lost on him. She'd resorted to cleavage-revealing tops and multiple (casual) peek-a-boo bend-overs both for the frontal and rear views, with no effect. And when she'd grabbed his ass a few times during some marathon makeout sessions, he'd merely chuckled. Not exactly the effect she'd been going for.

Dave returned to her side with a glass of champagne and a vodka with lime. Thank God. She downed the vodka.

"Is that for you?" she asked, pointing to the champagne.

"I wasn't sure which one you wanted, so I got both." He took the seat next to her. "I'm not having anything since I'm driving."

Steph downed the champagne too. Unfortunately, while it did help her forget about her poor crushed toes stuffed into silver Louboutin stilettos, it also had the effect of making her horny. She looked at Dave, who returned her gaze steadily. He had beautiful deep blue eyes behind those black-rimmed glasses. He was a middle school math teacher—a sweet, geeky, perfect gentleman. Dave was definitely not her usual type. But when he kissed her, he put heart and soul into it, and it was scorching hot. She'd found that out after their first date. The problem was—his hands never roamed. She would really like them to roam. It had been too long she'd gone untouched. So long she was almost pure again. A virgin in reverse. She giggled to herself.

"Would you like to dance again?" he asked. "I'm better at the slow songs."

"That's not saying much," she blurted. *Inhibitions down, honesty up*.

He frowned, and she kissed that frowny face. "Let's do the no-pants boogie," she said.

At his confused expression, she made a small poke-the-finger-in-the-hole-multiple-times gesture at him. Still confused. The hell with subtlety. "Let's do it."

His eyes widened behind his glasses. "You mean like…" His face flushed, and he glanced around at the people dancing nearby. "Like, right now?"

She smiled at him dreamily, running her fingers through the silky dark brown hair at the nape of his neck. "Yes."

He tugged on his tie. "But wouldn't you be more comfortable in a bed?"

Dave was so sweet, thinking of her comfort. She nipped his earlobe, and he jolted.

"After the reception, okay?" she whispered in his ear before she licked his earlobe and blew lightly across it. He held himself very still, and she wasn't sure if she'd pushed him away or reeled him in. "A bed sounds great," she added.

"That would be acceptable to me as well," he said in a strained voice.

Just then the reception got rowdy as a disco ball spun and the DJ blasted "Saturday Night Fever" by the Bee Gees. She laughed, watching Bare's antics with his John Travolta imitation. The man was a natural performer. He grabbed Amber and spun her onto the dance floor with him. Everyone flocked to join them.

"Come on," she said, slipping off her heels.

Dave followed her onto the dance floor, giving her lots of space as she danced with one finger pointing up and down in the air. He smiled, just watching her. She boogied all around him, using him much like a stripper pole. *This works much better*, she thought, *less toe crunching*. One disco song followed another and Dave made an excellent pole—sturdy, steady, warm. She was all over him, spinning around him, leaning into him, hanging off him, wrapping her leg around his and swaying. But then "YMCA" by The Village People played, and she had to stop working the pole to do the hand motions.

She'd just gotten to the "A" when he took her hands in his, bringing them down from over her head to the front of her. "Steph, meeting you was the best thing that ever happened to me."

She smiled and kept dancing. "Thanks, Dave!" she hollered over the music. She did the Y again and the M, missed the C, and jumped in again with the A.

"I really mean that." A lock of hair fell over his forehead.

She smiled and pushed his hair back into its side part just as the song hit the chorus. The crowd joined in, singing at the top of their lungs, drowning out Dave's next words.

"What? I can't hear you!" Steph shouted above the crowd.

"I said I love you!" he shouted.

"Oh!" She stopped dancing in her surprise. Before she could reply, he kissed her. His hands cradled her face as his mouth claimed hers in that slow, thorough way of his. The rowdy music and dancing faded away as heat flooded her. His tongue mated with hers, and she fisted her hands in his hair, wishing fervently his hands would move to other very interested parts of her body.

He released her, and she gazed at him—at his side part, his sweet turned-on face, right down to his navy suit with the New Balance sneakers. Through the haze of champagne and vodka and lust, it hit her with the same shock as her evil cat, Loki, leaping on her head in the middle of the night. Dave was a keeper. She loved him.

She opened her mouth to tell him so. He put his finger to her lips. "You don't have to say anything. I don't expect you to say it just because I did. I just wanted you to know."

She bit his finger.

"Ow!"

"I love you too, you big dork." That earned her another kiss.

Dave pulled back, and they gazed into each other's eyes. She beamed at him.

He grinned. "Fantastic."

"Yes!" Then she danced some more, using him as her personal stripper pole again. She was five foot ten and loved that she could actually look up at him without the heels. It made her feel less Amazon-like. He watched her with half-hooded eyes. She couldn't wait for after the reception. She was sure Dave would be just as slow and thorough in bed as he was when he kissed her. That could be very, very good. Many disco songs and a lot of champagne later, she left the reception hand-in-hand with Dave.

She floated on a happy cloud as Dave pulled her along to his car, practically running. Boy, someone was in a hurry. She giggled to herself. Something was nagging at her brain. Like a hornet circling her head, waiting to sting. Something she needed to tell Dave.

She frowned. Griffin. She needed to tell him about Griffin.

Dave opened the car door for her, but before she could get in, he pressed her against the side of the car and gave her a scorching kiss that made her want to rip his suit off and muss up his neat hair. Just when she was wrapping her leg around his, he broke the kiss.

She put her leg down. "I like your enthusiasm," she told him, planting a smacking kiss on his clean-shaven cheek. He turned, meeting her lips for another scorching kiss, and she forgot all about Griffin.

He stepped back, and she wobbled a bit.

His eyebrows scrunched down adorably. "How much have you had to drink?"

She'd lost count. This lovely tuxedoed waiter had been hovering around the dance floor. He always seemed to be there when her glass was empty. "Mostly champagne. I'm fine. Let's go back to my place. It's time you saw the inside." She giggled over her little joke. Dave would see the inside of her apartment and her. Yay!

He nodded slowly, looking a little too serious for her giddy state. He loved her! She loved him! Tonight was the night!

They drove the few blocks to an old Victorian in Clover Park that had been converted into apartments. She grabbed his hand and led him to her upstairs apartment. Once inside, she launched herself into his arms. "Take me, Dave, I'm yours."

～

Dave groaned as he wrapped his arms around Steph and wished he didn't have a conscience. He'd been hard from the moment he'd seen Steph in this curve-fitting dress with the stiletto heels. His eyes had done multiple tours of her ample cleavage, her narrow waist, and the curve of her hips leading down to those long legs in stilettos. Honestly, he'd been hard from the very first moment they met at that teachers' conference. Steph taught fifth grade and had attended his workshop on preparing fifth graders for middle school with the new math standards. Steph was gorgeous—long, silky brown hair, hazel eyes, full pouty lips, and that body. Any guy would want her. But the biggest turn-on for him was her brain. Steph had graduated *summa cum laude* from Columbia. Their children would be beautiful and smart.

But he'd taken things slow because, after a few encounters in his past that left him feeling unsatisfied, he'd decided he would only sleep with a woman if they loved each other. Not like when he'd slept with Sherri after two dates, only to discover her divorce was actually a separation that her husband was unaware they were having. And definitely not like when he'd been the rebound guy for Lisa, which he'd discovered after a hot all-night marathon of sex. She'd informed him in a note on his nightstand that he'd been the perfect antidote to her ex's sleaziness, and her faith in men had been restored. *Nice guy strikes again*, he thought wryly. He'd restored her faith so well that she'd left him and ventured back into the dating pool.

In any case, waiting for a meaningful encounter hadn't been too difficult. He tended to collect more women friends than girlfriends because he was the guy women confided in but didn't feel *that way* about. Tonight, to his delight, he'd discovered that what he'd hoped for between him and Steph was, in fact, true.

She was smiling up at him, waiting he supposed for him to "take" her, but her eyes weren't focused, and her speech earlier had been slightly slurred. He stroked her hair and let himself imagine for a moment her hair spread out on a pillow as he drove into her. He clamped down on that thought. *Ice bath, infinite snowballs heading his way, parent-teacher confer-ences.* That worked. He loved his job, even loved the rowdy middle school students, but dealing with the parents, especially those that didn't understand why Bobby couldn't get an A without turning in any homework, were the worst part of his job.

Gently, he set Steph a foot away from him. He looked around her apartment for the first time. He'd declined Steph's previous invitations to come up for a cup of coffee, which always followed a goodnight kiss while she squeezed his ass, because he wanted to be sure it was more than a one-time hookup. Finally, they were on the same page. If only Steph wasn't sloshed when he'd discovered she loved him too. Steph's apartment looked like those Pottery Barn catalogs his sister was forever poring over—wood coffee table with a silver bowl full of fake oranges, a red velvet blanket thrown over one side of a beige sofa.

He reached down to stroke a gray tabby cat that was rubbing against his leg. Steph's dress hit the floor. He jerked upright.

She was killing him. She looked like a lingerie model—light purple strapless bra with matching lace panties, still wearing the heels that screamed *I am very fuckable.* Her words rang through his head, *Take me, take me, take me.*

He grabbed the blanket from the sofa and covered her with it, wishing with every fiber of his being that he'd taken the opportunity to get her into bed before. He mentally slapped himself. What had he been thinking? Who cared about meaningful sex when a guy like him had a chance with a stunning (and smart) woman like her? For a smart guy, that had been a really stupid move.

"Da-aa-ave, I'm too hot for a blanket," she said as he guided her toward a half-open door that he figured was her bedroom.

"I know."

Ice and snow, ice and snow.

He gently pushed her onto the bed. The blanket parted in front, and he focused on her feet. Those slender feet in heels.

"I love you, David Olsen," Steph said in a soft breathy voice that made him break out in a sweat.

Maybe he could sober her up with coffee. He berated himself for bringing her that vodka when she'd asked. He glanced up at her face. Her eyes were already closing.

"I love you too," he said in a husky voice.

He pulled off the heels and stroked the top of her feet, feeling guilty about the red marks from the toe-stepping he'd done on the dance floor. She stretched out those long legs and sighed. He bit back a groan.

"I have to tell you about..." She curled up on her side, giving him an eyeful of curvy ass in lace panties. Just kill him now.

He yanked the comforter over her. "About what? Steph?"

She was sound asleep.

It sucked to be a gentleman.

2

Steph invited her friend Jasmine to come over the next day in a desperate cry for help. The moment her friend stepped into her apartment, Steph blurted, "I need a divorce."

Jaz's mouth dropped open in a perfect O of surprise. She pulled Steph to the sofa. "Back it up. Say what? I didn't know you were married!"

Steph grimaced over Jaz's volume. "Technically, I am."

Her friend crinkled her nose. "Does your boyfriend know?"

"You see the problem."

Jaz's brown eyes looked huge. "Uh, yeah?"

Jaz was a super-expressive, super-animated person. Maybe not the best choice to confide in on a hangover day, but Amber had already left for a quick honeymoon weekend getaway to Cape May. So that left Jaz. Jaz and Amber were the only two in the world she could trust with this delicate situation.

"So what's your husband think of your boyfriend and vice versa?" Jaz asked.

Steph shook her head and instantly regretted the movement. "I tried to tell Dave last night, but things got a little hazy after the vodka and the champagne." *And the kissing,* she added silently.

Jaz tucked a leg under her. "I told you to slow down on the champagne."

Steph blinked. She'd been so wrapped up in Dave, she hadn't spent much time with Jaz at the reception. Bare and Amber had invited the entire cast and crew from the Eastman summer community theater where they'd first gotten together. Steph usually played in the chorus, and Jaz was the choreographer.

"I have no memory of that," Steph said, rubbing her forehead. "Did you have a good time last night?"

"I had fun dancing, but ya know, that's my thing." She tossed her curly dark brown hair over her shoulder. "Back to you."

"How's the dance studio?" Steph asked.

Jaz smacked her arm. "Girl, don't tell me you're married and make small talk. Spill."

"I need water." Steph helped herself to a glass of water in the kitchen.

Jaz was right behind her. "I'll make you some green tea. All those antioxidants and just a pinch of caffeine work great for a hangover." She set the kettle on to boil. "So-oo, how long have we been married?"

"Five years."

Jaz's hands flew to her temples, eyes wide in shock. "Five years!"

Steph winced.

Jaz dropped her hands and lowered her voice. "Sorry. Five years? Where is this mystery man?"

Steph took a long drink of water. "He's in L.A. last I heard. We've been separated for most of that time, but neither of us ever bothered to officially call it off."

Jaz shook her head with a small smile as if she couldn't quite believe it. Steph mostly tried not to think about her failed marriage in her day-to-day life. She'd moved on, even without the official paperwork.

"Jaz, last night Dave said the L word. And I said it back and meant it." She met Jaz's eyes, looking for judgment, but saw only sympathy.

"You have to tell Dave right away," Jaz said. "Deception is not the way to go. Dave's a *nice* guy. There's not too many of those out there."

Steph watched Jaz get out the stuff for tea and mentally reviewed her night. She vaguely remembered going back to her apartment. Dave walking with her to the bedroom. Then nothing. She'd woken up in her underwear, the blanket tucked around her. Dave had neatly folded her dress and left it on her dresser. For a moment, she'd thought maybe they'd fooled around, but came to the conclusion that Dave would never take advantage like that. They'd spent six weeks just kissing. He was the real deal. Dave was the reason she desperately wanted this divorce. She was terrified that if she told Dave she was still married, his gentlemanly code of honor might make him leave her on moral grounds. She should be glad he was that kind of man. It meant he'd always choose the high ground. He'd never cheat on her. Yet he might think she was cheating on Griffin. Not that Griff was Mr. Squeaky Clean himself. What with all the groupies and supermodels.

"I'm not a totally horrible person, am I?" Steph asked. "I filed for divorce the first chance I got after I met Dave. Before that it never seemed to matter since things never moved past a couple of dates." Her throat got tight. "I knew right away Dave was special."

Jaz turned. "Wait. You already filed for divorce? Then what's the problem?"

"Griffin hasn't signed the papers. I have no idea why."

Jaz's eyebrows scrunched together. "That's weird. Do you think he wants to stay married?"

"If he does, he has a funny way of showing it. He hasn't picked up the phone in years. I mean, I know he travels a lot, but it's not hard to call or text." She closed her eyes as her headache took a turn for the worse, a pounding in her head to go along with the ache.

Jaz put a hand on her arm. "Are you okay? You don't look so good."

"I feel like shit."

"Lie down on the sofa. I'll bring the tea when it's ready."

Steph gratefully headed for the sofa, flopped down, and threw an arm over her eyes.

A short while later, Jaz brought the tea. The medicine Steph had taken earlier finally kicked in. She slowly sat up. "Thanks."

"Call Griffin after you finish your tea. I'll be your backup. If he doesn't listen"—Jaz made a fist—"I'll let him have it."

Steph found herself smiling. Jaz didn't even know Griff, but she was willing to step up for her. Unlike Steph, Jaz didn't back down from confrontation.

The moment she finished her tea, Jaz handed Steph her purse and ordered, "Call Griffin."

Steph pulled out her phone and stared at it. Griff had changed his cell number years ago and never bothered to give her the new one. "I don't have his number anymore. I just contact his manager."

"His manager?"

Steph hesitated before admitting, "I'm married to Griffin Huntley."

Jaz's jaw dropped. "Omigod! Griffin Huntley from Twisted Star? Griffin Huntley"—her voice hit a decibel that only dogs could hear—"the rock star?"

Steph cringed and lowered her hand, asking for a voice that didn't shatter glass. And her eardrums.

Jaz did a quick, excited foot-stomping dance from her seat on the sofa. "I love Twisted Star! You and Griffin Huntley! Omigod, how did that happen?"

Steph lifted one shoulder up and down. "I met him before he was famous. He was my guitar teacher. He taught private lessons on the side while he played gigs with his band, hoping to make it big. And then he did."

"And then he left you." Jaz squeezed her arm to soften the words.

"Yup. He got the big contract, went on tour, and never came back. We kept in touch that first year, doing the long-distance thing, but his calls got further and further apart until they just stopped." She twirled a piece of her hair. "I guess some part of me was hoping he'd come back, and we'd pick up where we left off."

Jaz gave her a sympathetic look. Everyone knew Griff had his pick of women. The gossip mags splashed with pictures of her husband with supermodels should've killed any hope Steph had of a reconciliation, but Griff kept it alive with what he did for her younger brother. She pushed that thought aside. Their divorce was long overdue. And she'd do her best for her brother with or without Griff's help.

Steph went on. "I just never met anyone that mattered enough to really push the issue of a divorce until—"

"Dave."

"Dave." She sighed.

Jaz shook her head with a smile. "Could Dave be any more different from Griffin?"

The two men were like Ashley Wilkes to Rhett Butler. Then who was Scarlett? Definitely not her. Griff sure liked attention like that Southern belle, and he had long black hair. She giggled, picturing her tattooed ex as the beautiful Scarlett.

"Maybe that's why it works between us," Steph finally said.

"You've got to be the squeaky wheel and keep following up with Griffin's manager. That's the only way this'll happen." Jaz looked her in the eye. "You can't leave Dave in the dark either. That's not fair to him. Tell him right away."

She was right. Steph knew she was right.

"Call Griffin's manager first," Jaz said. "Then tell Dave you want to see him tonight, and you'll tell him in person."

"Yes, Bossy Pants."

Jaz smiled. "That's Miss Bossy Pants to you."

Dave arrived at the brownstone in Brooklyn he'd grown up in and bent to kiss his grandmother on the cheek. "Happy birthday, Nonna." He handed her a card. Inside was a gift card to her favorite restaurant, Nathan's Famous (Famous for hot dogs).

"Thank you, sweetie. Are you hungry?"

His Italian grandmother felt it was her life's mission to feed him and his older sister, Christina. Only Chris refused to stuff herself on their grandmother's behalf. His sister was petite like their mother's Italian side while he was tall and lean like his father's Norwegian ancestors.

"Always," he said.

"There he is, my genius," his mom said, coming in from the kitchen and hugging him.

Dave winced. "Ma, I'm not a genius."

She ruffled his hair. "Some would say differently."

Dave smoothed his hair back into its side part. "Where's Dad?"

"He stopped by your Aunt Helen's house to see why her car keeps stalling."

His dad was a master mechanic, a skill he'd passed on to Dave from the age of five when he could first hold a wrench. Dave had considered following in his dad's footsteps, but his mom was adamant that he and his sister be the first in their family to go to college. He'd started out in mechanical engineering because of his affinity for machines, but was soon lured in by the beauty and elegance of mathematics. He'd gotten sidetracked after his master's degree by a two-year stint in Teach for America, teaching math to inner-city middle schoolers. He loved teaching—felt like he was making a real difference—and never looked back.

"There you are, Waldo," Chris said, coming down the stairs. She wore a purple velvet jogging suit, her usual attire when she wasn't working as a nurse.

He ignored her teasing about his glasses because he wanted to talk to her later about Steph. "Hey. After I eat, let's go for a drive." They still had a couple of hours before they had his grandmother's birthday dinner and cake.

"I'd love to get out of this place," Chris said.

"I heard that," their mom said from the sofa where she'd picked up her crochet—another blanket. He hoped it wasn't for him. He already had three in his closet.

"I've been here for two days." Chris threw up her hands. "I'm starting to feel like a shut-in."

Chris was thirty-two and had recently gone through a bitter divorce. Since then, she frequently spent her weekends off back home.

Their mom gestured to the door with her crochet needle. "So go, what do I care?"

"Ma, don't be like that," Chris said, throwing an arm around him. "It's just sibling bonding time."

Their mom smiled. "You two are close now that you're grown up. Didn't I tell you he wouldn't always be an annoying little twerp?"

"Yeah, you did." Chris reached up to ruffle his hair, and he smoothed it back in place. "Now he's just an annoying big twerp."

He scooped her up and turned her upside down.

"Aah! Put me down!"

"Not unless you call me King Dave for the rest of the day."

"Never!"

"I can stand here all day." He glanced down. Her face was turning an interesting shade of red.

"Okay! Put me down, King Dave!"

He set her back upright on the floor. She immediately kicked him in the shin. "Ow!"

"Children!" his mom said.

He limped into the kitchen. Nonna piled a plate with leftover roast beef and a side of ziti and put it in the microwave. He dug in a few minutes later at the small kitchen table.

Chris sat across from him and watched him eat. "You know we're having manicotti and cake in two hours."

"If the boy wants to eat, let him eat," Nonna said as she covered the leftover food with aluminum foil.

"Where do you put it all?" Chris asked. "You're always thin."

He chewed for a moment. "I run."

She scoffed. "I run too. If I just look at pasta, I gain five pounds."

"High metabolism?"

"You suck."

He pointed his fork at her. "You suck, King Dave."

She snorted.

"It wouldn't hurt you to put a little meat on your bones, Christina Marie," Nonna said. "Men like curves."

"I got curves," Chris said. "I don't need love handles."

"More to love," Dave quipped.

He finished the meal, thanked his grandmother, and pulled out his car keys. "Let's go."

Chris slid into the passenger side of his Ford Fusion Hybrid—he loved its fuel efficiency—and promptly changed the radio to a top-forty station. He didn't even change it back to National Public Radio (though NPR was doing a fascinating segment on game theory as it applied to online algorithms). Nothing could spoil his mood now that he was in love with someone that loved him back.

"I met someone," he told her.

"Seriously?"

He glanced at her. It shouldn't have been that shocking. He wasn't an ogre.

"Yes, seriously," he said. "Her name is Stephanie Moore. She's a fifth grade teacher. I'm crazy about her. I'm thinking of proposing."

"Whoa, slow down there. How long have you been dating?"

"Six weeks. I love her. She said she loves me too."

"Six weeks isn't very long. How well do you know her?"

He stopped at a stop sign and gestured to some kids to cross the street. "I'm thirty years old. I know what I want. I know she's the one. Do you think the Diamond District is open today?" It was Sunday, but some of the shops might be open. New York City was hopping every day of the week.

"It's too soon to shop for diamonds! You're rushing things. Just because you sleep with someone doesn't mean you have to run out and buy them a ring. I sure never got that."

He didn't comment on the sleeping-together thing. They'd get there. Maybe tonight. Or tomorrow since they both were off for Columbus Day. As for the ring, Chris might be right. He didn't want to scare Steph off. On the other hand, Chris was still bitter about her ex divorcing her to marry his pregnant girlfriend, so she was probably not the best person to ask for diamond-ring advice.

He turned down a street that went past his old elementary school. "Okay, I'll skip the Diamond District. I'll research diamonds online, just in case."

"I'm telling you—*too soon.*"

He thought of last night, how Steph had said she loved him. How she'd said "I love you" a second time before she fell asleep. He found himself smiling.

"Are you sure she'll say yes?" Chris asked quietly.

He grinned. "Yes."

"Well, now I've got to meet her. She must be something awfully special."

"She is, she really is." Then he proceeded to tell her all of Steph Moore's many virtues.

Steph made sure to ask for a back booth for lunch with Dave at Garner's Sports Bar & Grill the next day. Last night he'd called when he got home from Brooklyn, but she'd already been in her pajamas, exhausted from the previous night's partying. Knowing she needed to have their big talk, she'd put him off until today. She wanted this relationship to work, wanted to see where things could go. She was rusty on relationships, but she knew Jaz was right—honesty was the most important thing. She'd spent the morning going over possible ways to break the news, but there really was no good way to tell your steady boyfriend that you still had a husband. That was probably why she made it through the entire lunch without a peep about Griffin.

"You're awfully quiet," Dave said. "Everything okay?" He pushed the last sliver of their shared dessert of apple pie toward her. "Let's split it. Pi divided by two means you're the one." He grinned and waggled his brows.

Another math joke. He meant the number pi divided by two equaled one. She shook her head, a smile tugging at her lips. "Those pi jokes never get old."

He smiled. "That's why I always order it."

"I'm full. You eat it."

She watched him eat and tried to calm the jitters in her stomach. She just had to say it. Dave would understand. Hopefully.

She took a deep breath. "Dave, we need to talk."

He straightened up. "That sounds ominous."

"No…it's…I don't know." She blew out a breath, suddenly at a loss for words. How did you tell the man you loved that you were married?

He set down his fork. "You're making me nervous. Are you breaking up with me?"

A hysterical laugh escaped. "No!"

He flopped back in his seat. "Good. Because after all the I love yous…" He gestured back and forth between them.

"I know, right?" She laughed maniacally and clamped her mouth shut.

He became serious, leaning forward to study her across the table. "I'm glad."

"Sorry. I mean, me too." She barked out a laugh. "I'm sorry. This isn't funny." She forced herself to stop the insane smiling. "It's just so hard to talk about."

He took her hand. "Steph, I love you." His thumb rubbed small circles across her palm, warming her. "You can tell me anything."

He was so fucking sweet, and she was going to ruin everything. She felt sick. "Oh, God…"

He squeezed her hand. "It's okay. Just say it."

"I'm married," she blurted, then all in a rush, "I filed for divorce after I met you, but Griffin hasn't signed the papers."

His eyes widened. He dropped her hand and leaned back from the table as if to get away from her words. "You're *married*?"

She grimaced. "Only technically. We've been separated almost the entire five years."

Hurt washed over his face, and she felt that like a stab to the heart. She hated that she'd put that look there.

He stared at the table. "Technically married is still married."

"It's not a real marriage," she said. "It's over."

He still wouldn't look at her. "You said you loved me," he said quietly.

Her heart lurched painfully. "I do."

"I was planning…I thought…" He met her eyes with a hard look. "I'm so stupid." His face flushed red with anger. "When were you planning on telling me?"

"I don't know." Her hands fluttered helplessly in the air. "Now, I guess. When it seemed like we might actually have a future."

"She's married," he muttered to himself. *"Married."* He took off his glasses and pinched the bridge of his nose. He stayed like that for a long time.

"Dave? I just wanted you to know. Honesty is important."

He grunted.

"We can still be together."

He finally slid his glasses back in place and met her eyes. "I don't know about this." He exhaled sharply. "I wish you'd just been honest with me from the beginning."

"I know. I definitely should've been more upfront."

It was just that she hated confrontations. It was something she knew she had to work on, but years of trying to be the easy, never-get-into-trouble kid for her single mom were ingrained into her. Her younger brother had been a lot of work for her mom. Even when Steph was at work, if a kid was acting up in her classroom, she'd just send them to the principal instead of confronting them on their behavior.

He rubbed the back of his neck. "Are you really getting a divorce?"

"Yes. As soon as I can arrange it."

He stared at the table. "I'm getting a really bad feeling about this. Your husband's not going to show up here and kick my ass, is he?"

She laughed much too hard. "No way! I haven't heard a

peep from him in five years! No way he'd be any threat to you."

His lips formed a flat line. "Okay. I don't like it, but..." He ran a hand through his hair, leaving it a rumpled mess. "I need some time to think about this."

"Okay. Take as much time as you need."

He nodded. "Ready to go?"

"Sure."

Dave left some bills on the table and drove her home. He was quiet, which made her feel jumpy. Maybe he was in shock. Just like always, he parked and walked her to the front door. She gave him a quick kiss goodbye, wondering if it was their last.

"See you later," she said.

"Yup," he said tersely before turning to go.

She let herself into her apartment, mad at herself for waiting so long to tell Dave the truth, but also mad at Griffin for not signing those damn divorce papers. She punched the number for Griff's manager, Bill, on her cell. She got his voicemail *again* and left a message, "This is Stephanie Moore-Huntley, Griffin's *wife*. Tell him if he doesn't sign those divorce papers right away, I will demand back alimony and take him for all he's worth!"

3

———

Griffin yawned and stretched as he slowly woke to the sound of his cell ringing. He would've ignored it, except the ringtone, Joan Jett's "I Love Rock 'n' Roll," meant it was his manager, Bill. He ignored those calls at his own peril. He sat up, disturbing the naked woman at his side, who pushed her long blond hair out of her face and gave him a sultry smile. He gave her a slow, sexy smile back. What was her name again? Jennifer. No, Jillian. Erica?

"I'll meet you poolside, sweetheart," he told her before taking the call. "What's up?"

He watched as the woman walked nude from the room, hips swaying, that sweet ass. She looked over her shoulder, caught him looking, and blew him a kiss. Bill was jabbering on about ticket sales, but all Griff could think was why the hell was he kicking this beautiful woman out of bed. Tanya. That was it. Tanya.

She disappeared from view. He headed naked to the bathroom to take a piss, phone still to his ear, as Bill bitched about sales for the band's latest album, Griff's cash flow, and the European tour. Blah, blah, blah. Griff had a manager so he didn't have to deal with all that business stuff. He was in it for the music. The lifestyle wasn't too shabby either.

He left the cell on the counter, not bothering to put it on

speaker or tell Bill to hold on. The man would just talk until he had nothing left to say. Then Griff would say okay, and they'd go about their respective jobs. He took care of business, washed his hands, and caught his reflection in the mirror. Bags under his eyes, dark rings indicating fatigue, and the wrinkle in his forehead was deeper. Damn, it sucked getting old. He was thirty-five, had hit the big time *finally* at thirty with his band Twisted Star, but the late nights and constant partying were catching up to him.

He picked up the phone—Bill was onto some legal complication with Griff's lawyer, Paulie D—grabbed a fresh pair of briefs, pulled them on, and headed to the kitchen for water and the frozen tea bags he used to get rid of the bags under his eyes. He stopped at the mention of Stephanie.

"What was that part about Stephanie?" he asked.

Bill let out a noisy exhale. "Were you listening at all? I heard you take a piss."

"Yeah, yeah, I was listening. I just wasn't sure I heard that part about Steph correctly."

"She's left several messages, and I know you don't want a divorce—"

"So why are we talking about her?" Griff liked having a wife. It helped deflect women looking for a commitment. *So sorry. Can't. I'm married.*

"She sounded really serious this time. She threatened to sue for back alimony. To, I quote, 'take him for all he's worth.'"

"That's weird." He grabbed a bottle of Perrier from the fridge and twisted off the cap. That wasn't like Steph to care about money. What was she really trying to say? Did she miss him? He'd been thinking about her more lately, back there in Connecticut, wondering how she was doing. Sometimes, on a rare night in, when he was alone, he wondered what his life would've been like if he'd stayed. If he was still a guitar teacher. They'd probably have a bunch of kids, barely able to make ends meet. Steph always wanted kids. He didn't. He knew what it was like to grow up poor, having the electricity shut off because your single mom couldn't pay the bill on a secretary's paycheck. His dad was also a musician, one that couldn't be nailed down in one place. Like father, like son.

He took a long drink and watched the blonde lounging by the pool turn over, sunbathing topless. Gretchen? Did she have an accent? He couldn't remember.

"Are you listening?" Bill demanded.

"Mmm," he murmured noncommittally. He got out the frozen tea bags and headed for the long white sectional sofa.

"I said go see Stephanie. See what's got a bug up her ass. Make sure we don't have a money problem here."

He stretched out on the sofa and put the bags over his eyes. "Why do I have to see her? Just wait until she takes legal action and sic Paulie D on her. He'll take care of everything."

"Can I be honest with you here, Griff?"

"Sure."

"You need the publicity. It's as simple as that. I've got a call in to Mandy. You're taking the jet tonight. I've arranged cars for both of you. We need pictures of you with your secret wife. It won't hurt her and, believe me, the mystery of your long-lost wife will only help you."

Griff grunted. Mandy worked for a trashy tabloid, *Stars Chronicle*, and had always reported on him in a flattering light. They were friendly. And he wasn't opposed to seeing Steph again. Their brief time together was the only time in his life he felt like part of a real family—the two of them and her younger brother, Joey. They'd lived together before he went on his first tour. He smiled, thinking of Joey. Sweet kid. Maybe he could squeeze in a visit to him too. It'd been a year since he'd last seen him.

"Yeah, sure," Griff said. "Looking forward to it."

"You are? Great!" Bill blew out a breath, muttering to himself, then louder, "I knew you'd come through when it counted. You've got until Saturday; then we need you back here for *The Bridgette Show*."

They had a gig on the popular late-night talk show. "No problem."

"Thatta boy."

Griff hung up and headed over to the pool. "Hey,

gorgeous, I gotta leave town. I'll call you, okay?"

The woman stood and grabbed her bikini top. "I'll wait by the phone," she said dryly with no accent.

"Michaela!" he said triumphantly. Her eyes flashed, and he quickly realized he should've kept that to himself.

"It's Taylor, asshole." She turned on her heel and stalked toward the house.

"Don't let the door hit your pretty ass on the way out, Taylor," he called after her.

She flipped him the bird and left.

He dropped his briefs and dove into the crystal blue water, thinking of his young bride, Steph, feeling younger already himself.

Steph dragged through work at Clover Park Elementary School the next day. She hadn't slept at all last night. She was afraid things were over with Dave before they really had a chance. Not surprisingly, she hadn't heard from Griffin.

"I don't care how upset you are, you still need your sleep," Amber was saying as they headed toward the school's exit at the end of the day. She'd filled Amber in on all the latest over lunch in the teachers' lounge. Her friend taught art. "You have to take care of you. Don't make me get you into bed tonight." She paused and cocked her head to the side. "Wait. That didn't come out right."

Steph smiled weakly.

Amber opened the door and stopped short. "Uh, Steph, there's a limo. You don't think—"

Steph pushed past Amber and stared. The stretch limo looked incongruous sitting in the front parking lot of Clover Park Elementary next to the sea of minivans. Her stomach dropped. "No," she muttered like a curse.

The back limo door opened—black Converse sneakers followed by long legs encased in black leather, a black leather jacket, black aviator sunglasses. And that hair, that beautiful thick, wavy black hair. She'd always envied his hair.

"Omigod, it's Griffin Huntley!" Amber shrieked.

Steph's head whipped around to stare at her usually mellow, easygoing friend.

Amber shrugged. "It just slipped out. I've never seen a celebrity up close." Her voice dropped to a hushed whisper. "He's coming over."

Steph turned as Griff swaggered over. He smiled, revealing dazzling white teeth. Someone visited a Hollywood dentist. She didn't smile back.

He hugged her anyway. "Good to see you again, Steph."

"What are you doing here?" she demanded.

Amber elbowed her and said under her breath, "Introduce us."

"This is my friend Amber," Steph said automatically. "Amber, Griffin."

Amber went all shy. "Hi. I love your music."

Griff angled his body toward Amber and gave her friend a slow, sexy smile. "Thanks. It's always nice to meet a fan. Love the pink streaks." He indicated her hair.

Amber nodded and smiled, nodded and smiled. She looked like a bobblehead doll.

Steph waved a hand in front of Griff's face. He was always looking for an audience. He slowly pulled off his shades, blinked, and turned to her with those hazel eyes that matched her own. Her throat felt tight. She'd always thought their kids would've had hazel eyes.

He gave her that same sexy smile meant to charm.

She was long immune to his charms. "I hope you're here with the signed divorce papers."

"Is that any way to greet your husband?" He looked to Amber for her reaction to this puzzling event.

Amber took a step back. "I'd better go. Call me if you need anything, Steph."

Steph nodded.

Griff spoke in a silky whisper. "Shall we go?" He gestured to the limo.

She didn't move. "Do you have the signed papers?"

"I want to talk about it first. Come on, Steph, just give me a little time. I'll drive you home."

"My car's here."

"Then I'll follow you to your place."

She stood there for a moment, noticing the curious looks of her coworkers and parents as they made their way to their cars. "Fine."

She got into her sunny yellow VW Beetle and made the short drive home. What in the world could Griff possibly want to talk about after all these years? And why did he have to come in person? She knew exactly why she'd fallen for him when she was in her twenties—hello, hormones!—but now at thirty-two, her priorities had changed. It wasn't all about gorgeous hair and a killer bod. She wanted more—stability, faithfulness, children. She'd always wanted children. That kind of life was one thing she knew she could get with Dave.

On their first date, Dave had taken her to a hibachi restaurant for dinner. They'd sat around the huge hibachi grill with two families and had a blast watching the chef cook up dinner with all sorts of tricks like the flaming volcano made of onions, catching shrimp shells in his chef's hat, and flipping cucumber bits off his flipper into Dave's mouth. The fact that he'd taken her to a family-friendly place for their first date spoke volumes by itself, but then after, he'd driven her home, and they'd taken a walk through the backstreets of Clover Park. It had been summer, and lots of people were still out—walking their dogs, hanging out on their front porches. Kids were riding bikes and chasing fireflies. Dave had turned to her and said, "This must be a great place to raise a family."

She'd thought so too when she'd moved to town a few years before. "It would. You don't miss the city life?"

"It's fun when you're younger," he replied. "I mean, there's always stuff to do. But if I was married with kids, I'd like to raise them in a small town like this."

"Me too." They smiled at each other, and something about the tender look in his eyes told her it could happen for them. And for the first time in a long time, she felt hopeful about the future.

Now she parked in front of her place and noticed a black

sedan with tinted windows parked across the street. It didn't look like one of her neighbor's cars. Griff's limo pulled up behind her. She waited for him to get out.

"Friend of yours?" she asked, pointing across the street.

He shrugged. "I don't know anyone in Clover Park except you."

She tried to see through the front windshield of the strange car, but couldn't make out anyone. She turned and headed to the front door of the house, unlocking it. She went up the stairs to her apartment ahead of him, feeling sure he was checking out her ass. At least her skirt covered her decently. She glared at him over her shoulder as she caught him doing *exactly* what she suspected.

"What?" he asked in the voice of the innocent. His eyes sparkled mischievously.

"You know what."

He chuckled. She let him in and sat on the far end of the sofa, hugging a pillow, waiting for him to talk. He took his time, peeling off his leather jacket to reveal a snug black T-shirt. His muscular arms were covered in tattoos. He'd only had one tattoo when she'd known him—a heart on his bicep with her name in it. She checked. It was still there.

"I thought you'd have that one removed," she said, pointing to her name.

He gave her a slow once-over from her hair to her chest covered by the pillow and down her legs. Her irritation grew as his gaze slowly dragged back up, lingering on her mouth before flicking to her eyes. "Now why would I do that? You're my wife."

"Oh, and how does that go over with your groupies?" she sniped.

He took his time answering. She watched while he made himself comfortable on her sofa. Her cat, Loki, hissed and jumped off the sofa, then stalked from the room.

He spread his arms across the top of the cushions, taking up all the space. "It keeps away who I want it to keep away. My long-lost wife who still holds my heart." He patted the cushion next to him. "Come over here."

"No."

"Come on, Steph. I only bite if you say pretty please."

She threw the pillow at him. He laughed and slid over next to her.

"How've you been, darlin'?" he crooned, stroking a lock of her hair, his warm fingers grazing her neck.

She snatched her hair back. "Don't pull this crap with me. This isn't a seduction scene. I'm not one of your groupies. I—"

"That's right, Stephanie Moore-Huntley, you're my wife." His voice was low and husky, and she refused to be drawn in again.

She blew out an exasperated breath. "Griff, I met someone. I need to be single again. He doesn't like that I'm still married."

He stretched out his leather-clad legs. "Sounds like a conservative dweeb."

"He's not. Dave's wonderful. So sweet. A perfect gentleman." She found herself smiling, thinking of Dave.

Griff gave her a disbelieving look. "So you just expect me to step aside and let this wuss take my place."

"Stop calling him names. He treats me right. I love him."

Griff sat up straight. "You're serious, aren't you?"

"Yes!"

Does he think this whole divorce thing is some kind of ploy to get his attention?

He looked hurt. "I came back here hoping to give us another chance."

She felt like grabbing him by the hair and shaking him. "We haven't lived together in *five* years."

"It's been that long? Huh." He stared off in the distance, thinking as hard as his pea brain could. "I want to meet him."

She narrowed her eyes. "Why?"

"I want to meet the man who's taking my place."

"That's ridiculous."

"I've got until Saturday before I have to be back in L.A. for a gig. Tell Dave I want to meet him, and then I'll sign the papers." He smiled smugly.

She barely resisted smacking that smug smile off his face. "Do you have the papers with you?"

"Nah. They're in L.A. with Paulie D."

That was his lawyer. That meant he wouldn't sign them until after he left. She'd have to take his word for it that he would. But what choice did she have? She needed to move on with her life.

"Fine," she snapped. She reached for her purse on the floor, pulled out her cell, and dialed Dave. Thankfully she got him and not his voicemail. She spoke fast. "Hi, it's Steph. Don't be mad, but Griffin showed up today. I had no idea he was coming."

"Hi, Dave," Griff called cheerfully.

Steph covered Griff's mouth with her hand, and he flicked his tongue rapidly over her palm. She quickly dropped her hand and gave him a death stare. "He says he wants to meet you before he signs the divorce papers. Could you *please* come over? I would really, really appreciate it." She held her breath. "Okay. Bye."

"What did he say?" Griff asked.

"He's coming right over."

Griff rubbed his hands together in anticipation. "Good. So now what?"

"What do you mean?"

"What should we do until he gets here?" He gave her a slow, sexy smile that infuriated her.

"You should just sit there and think about how you're going to treat Dave with the respect he deserves. I'm going to call a friend. And don't answer the buzzer. I'll do it." She headed for her bedroom.

"Love it when you're bossy, wife," he called.

She looked over her shoulder to find him texting. Probably to one of his harem. She slammed the bedroom door behind her. She heard his low laugh and groaned in aggravation. This might all be a game to him, but she was serious, and damn if she was going to let him turn her life upside-down.

She was about to call Amber—Jaz would still be teaching dance class—when her eye caught on the framed picture of her and her younger brother, Joey, on the nightstand. She grabbed the picture, sank to the bed, and stared at her cheerful brother. Joey was twenty-eight and had Down syndrome. He lived at Horizon Village, a private community for adults with Down syndrome. He loved it there and often spoke with pride of his job cleaning hotel rooms and the nights he was in charge of dinner at his group home (with the help of the house mother).

Griff was the one that paid the tuition.

Joey was the only reason she'd held out hope for so long that Griff might still love her, might still come back to her. Not only did Griff pay the tuition, every celebrity charity event he did, he sent all the proceeds to Horizon Village. She'd never asked him to do any of that.

Shortly after she married Griff, her mother had lost a long battle with breast cancer. She suspected her mom had held on just long enough to see her daughter married. Her dad had left right after Joey's birth, unable to handle having a son with special needs. So that left Steph to care for Joey. Her mom had spoken often of Horizon Village as a way for Joey to live as an independent adult and for Steph to live her own life. When her mom got sick, her mom put Joey on a long waiting list for scholarship residents.

In the meantime, Joey had lived with her and Griff for the first few months of their marriage at her mom's house. Then Griff got that big recording contract, and the first thing he did was hand her a check for the first year of Joey's tuition. They'd moved her brother into his new home, and Steph had spent the next three months by Griff's side as he toured. Then his music video went viral, his popularity exploded, and he sent Steph home to wait as his tour went global. He'd said it would be a grueling pace, and he wanted her to relax at home. He wanted her to go back to her job before she lost it, in case this rock 'n' roll gig didn't pan out. And he'd promised regular visits.

That was the beginning of the end.

She had to tread carefully with Griff. She knew he'd prepaid the next two years of Joey's tuition with the winnings from his last celebrity poker tournament. Would he keep paying the tuition out of consideration for her? Would Joey be upset if he had to move in with her and leave the people he felt so comfortable with? He had friends there. Would she be able to handle a life spent caring for her brother and still live her own life? Would Dave want any part of that?

She dropped her head in her hands. It didn't matter. She couldn't hold back because of what might happen. She'd handle it. Her marriage wasn't real. It was time to end it. She made a quick call to Amber to fill her in and to calm herself. A short time later, she heard the buzzer, and her heart raced. Dave was here.

Dave drove like a maniac from Eastman where he'd just finished up his extra-help session for some students after school. He couldn't believe the hold this guy Griffin held over Steph. Like he had any right after a five-year separation. He'd spent most of the night going over Steph's shocking news, reminding himself this was nothing like Sherri, this was a real separation, but still feeling uneasy about it. And really not happy about the dishonesty. Were there other things she'd kept from him? A relationship couldn't work without honesty.

But, dammit, when she called and he heard the pleading in her voice, the near desperation, he knew he had to show up at her place. He could tell she didn't want to be alone with Griffin. He would go because she needed him.

Hell, who was he kidding? He loved her. He missed her after just one day of being apart. Him showing up at Steph's place would help her. Griffin would sign the divorce papers, and Steph would be free to live her life. With him.

He pulled up to her place, parking on the street behind a stretch limo. A prickling of unease went through him. Was Steph's husband a multimillionaire? He got out of his Ford Fusion and walked briskly up the steps. So what if her husband was rich? Money wasn't everything. Steph wouldn't care about that. They were both teachers. She understood the intangible rewards of teaching, like that moment when a student's face lit up as they grasped a new concept. Those moments were gold.

He hit the intercom. "It's Dave."

"Come on up," Steph said, buzzing him in the front door.

He took the stairs two at a time, smoothed his hair, and knocked.

The door swung open. "You got here fast," Steph said.

"I might have broken the speed limit a few times," he admitted. He was usually careful never to break any traffic laws. He'd never even gotten a ticket before.

She kissed him on the cheek. "I missed you," she whispered.

His chest ached. "I missed you too."

A voice drawled from the sofa. "Aww…isn't that sweet?"

Dave strode in to meet the man who stood between him and his woman. The other man stood, nearly as tall as Dave, but with more bulk. There was something familiar about the guy—the leather, the tattoos, the long hair. *Shit.*

"You're Griffin Huntley," Dave said. He only knew this disturbing fact because his sister, Christina, was a Twisted Star fanatic. Chris went to all of their concerts on the East Coast. She even had a poster of Griffin in her bedroom like a teenaged girl.

Griffin flashed a smile that held little warmth. "In the flesh."

Dave turned to Steph in horror. "Your husband is a freaking rock star?"

Steph put a hand on his arm. "It's no big deal."

"And what do you do?" Griffin asked.

Dave stood tall and proud. "I'm a math teacher."

Griffin raised a brow. "Sexy."

Dave saw red. What he did wasn't glamorous or sexy, but it was important work. And Steph, also a teacher, was the woman he loved. How dare Griffin put down both of them in their chosen professions? This guy probably wouldn't know a square root from a binomial.

He got in Griffin's face. "You got a problem with teachers? Because in case you hadn't noticed, Steph and I are both teachers."

"I don't got a problem with teachers," Griffin shot back. He put his hands on Dave's chest and gave him a shove. "I got a problem with a guy horning in on my woman."

Dave shoved back, but Griffin didn't budge. *Dammit.* He vowed to begin lifting weights this weekend. "Then there's no problem because she's not your woman."

"Maybe we should take this outside," Griffin said, challenge in his eyes.

Steph stepped between them. "Enough! Griff, you've met Dave, so now you can sign the papers. I won't ask for a cent from you."

Griffin eyed Dave. "I'm not losing my wife to a geek like you."

"She deserves better than a player like you," Dave spat.

He'd seen Griffin on plenty of tabloid covers at the supermarket with models in bikinis. Steph was more beautiful than any of them. This guy was a complete and total moron not to see what he'd had in Steph. Plus she was smart and nice, which was also important to a guy seeking a partner, not just a fuck buddy, though he still wanted to be both to Steph. Badly. *Dammit.* Why did Griffin have to show up before Dave had managed to get Steph into bed? Him and his stupid morals. What kind of chance did he stand against a famous rock star? Rock stars could do whatever the hell they wanted and get away with it.

He was still mentally berating himself when Griffin snapped his fingers right in Dave's face. Dave met his eyes and scowled.

Griffin crossed his arms. "I said," he drawled, "game on, *geek.*"

Dave's hackles rose. He was very competitive and always won the online chess and scrabble games he played with the best players the Internet had to offer. "Game fucking on!"

"Dave!" Steph exclaimed.

Dave glanced at her and went back to staring down his

opponent. "I'm not afraid of a little competition." Bluffing was very important in one-on-one male confrontations. He lifted his chin to look down at the enemy. "I was a mathlete in high school."

Griffin burst out laughing.

Dave shoved him. Caught off guard, Griffin stumbled back.

"You'll pay for that," Griffin said, charging toward Dave.

Dave quickly took refuge behind the sofa. Griffin leaped over it, grabbed him, and they hit the floor with a thud.

"Griff!" Steph shouted. "Get off him this minute!"

"Ahh," Griffin moaned, grabbing one of Steph's hands. She had both her hands in his long hair and was pulling pretty hard if his eyelids lifting into weird, curving slits was any indication. He got off Dave, assisted by Steph's grip on his hair.

"Both of you get out," Steph said, hustling them toward the door. "There's a ridiculous amount of testosterone in here. I can't believe two grown men are acting this way."

Griffin grabbed his jacket. "This isn't over," he told Steph before walking out the door.

After the door shut behind Griffin, Dave turned to Steph to explain his manly display. "I can't let him treat you that way."

Steph shook her head. "Just go."

"I'm not giving up," Dave said fiercely. "He doesn't deserve you." He would fight for the woman he loved. And he would win.

"Bye, Dave." She pushed him through the doorway and shut the door in his face.

He stood there for a minute, calculating his chances of getting back into her apartment, decided they weren't good, and headed downstairs. Thankfully, the limo was already pulling away. He needed time to formulate a plan. The most romantic sweep-her-off-her-feet plan that didn't involve money or rock-star sex appeal.

That should come easily, he didn't have either.

4

———

Steph collapsed on her sofa with a Lean Cuisine for dinner later that night, completely dumbfounded that the two men in her life were actually fighting over her. First, the fact that Griff thought he even had a chance with her was laughable. No communication for years, and then he suddenly claimed his rights as a husband. Ha! And Dave going all caveman and in Griff's face was shocking. She'd never seen him act tough or macho the entire time she'd known him. He'd always been a perfect mild-mannered gentleman. What had gotten into him?

When she'd first met Dave at the state teachers' conference, he'd been running a workshop on the new math standards and how to implement them. Steph had felt it especially important to attend his workshop to prepare her fifth grade students for middle school math. He'd been adorable at the podium, wearing a navy blue T-shirt with a giant pi symbol on it. That had caught her attention right away in the sea of business-casual outfits. And he'd been so enthusiastic too, with big hand gestures as he spoke.

"Hi, I'm Mr. Olsen," he said with a wave, "but all of you past puberty can call me Dave."

She giggled. A teacher joke. The rest of the teachers stared blankly at Dave.

"Thank you," Dave said, pointing at her. "I'll be here for the next ninety minutes."

She smiled. He smiled back.

Dave cleared his throat. "Anyway, I heard it's always good to start a lecture with a joke, so here goes." His palms went up. "Why did the chicken cross the Moebius strip?"

"Why?" a man in the back row asked dryly.

"To get to the other...er, um..." He scratched his head.

Silence. Steph smiled.

Dave grinned. "Thank you smiling woman in the front row." He swept his arms forward. "Moving right along with number bonds..."

After the workshop, she'd approached him with a few others on the pretense of asking him a question. Up close, she liked his size, taller than her, his lean build with broad shoulders, the deep blue eyes she finally saw behind those black-rimmed glasses when it was nearly her turn to speak to him. He was cute. Geeky cute.

Finally, they were face to face.

"Hey," he said. "Thanks for humoring me. It was just crickets out there. It's like no one expects math to be fun." His brows crinkled comically at the notion.

"I hear ya," she said with a laugh, though she wasn't crazy about math. She did appreciate him lightening up what was typically a long day of dry, put-you-to-sleep workshops.

He grinned, and his blue eyes sparkled behind his glasses.

"Any advice on the best way to introduce proofs at the fifth-grade level to prepare my students for middle school?" she asked.

"I've got a lot to say on this subject." He looked at his shoes. "Do you, uh, want to grab some lunch, and we can, uh, talk about it?"

"I'd love to."

He met her eyes and grinned. "Great! What's your name?"

"Stephanie Moore."

He shook her hand and warmth shot up her arm at his touch. Their eyes met and held. He'd felt it too. The chemistry.

"Pleased to meet you, Stephanie," he said in a husky voice.

At Dave's suggestion, they went to a restaurant down the street from the hotel for a quieter atmosphere. Their lunch had been informative. Dave, true to his word, had a lot to say about proofs as well as preparing students for middle school math. She loved his enthusiasm for teaching. She discovered they worked for the same school district, which meant he lived not too far from her. She already knew she wanted to see him again.

They reached for the check at the same time, and they both blushed.

"I'll pay," Dave said. "As payment for listening to me yammer on."

"It was educational," she said.

A corner of his mouth kicked up. "That's me."

As they walked back to the hotel conference center, they chatted about the conference and the workshops they'd attended while Steph kept wondering if he'd ask for her phone number.

He held the door to the hotel open for her like a perfect gentleman. They were about to rejoin the masses for the afternoon workshops when Steph did something she'd never done in her life. She asked him out.

"You want to have dinner this weekend?" she asked.

"You-you're asking me out? Wow. That would be awesome!" His smile was ear-to-ear, and she was glad she'd asked. "Give me your cell. I'll program my number in."

When he handed it to her, she glanced down. It read: Teacher Dave. She loved the way he was simply himself with no pretense, no pretending. A sweet guy who loved math, who wore what he wanted, who expressed exactly how he felt without hiding behind a macho guy façade. It was so refreshing.

Now, with Dave going toe-to-toe with Griff, she wasn't sure if the real Dave had come out of hiding or if he was pretending to be something he wasn't just to impress her.

Either way, she wanted the sweet Dave back. She had enough of testosterone overload with Griff.

She grabbed the TV remote and stilled. What was that noise? It sounded like singing. She walked to the back of her apartment toward her bedroom. Yup, singing and an acoustic guitar. She pushed up the window blinds and stared down at Griff gazing up at her. She should've known he wouldn't go away that easily. He never did listen to what she wanted. She opened her window. He was standing under the motion-sensor light in the back that was as bright as a spotlight. It was her favorite song of his—a ballad, "Once I Held You." He smiled as he sang:

You're hot like a dream
Girl, what you do to me
My insides melt like cream
What you do to me

Some of the other tenants came out to listen. Pete, a guy in his twenties, bobbed his head in time to the music. Someone in a hoodie stood next to Pete. Maybe his girlfriend? It was hard to tell, but the size of the person said woman. Roberta and Pauline, sisters who shared the first floor apartment, looked enthralled. Griff kept singing, right to her, his heart in his eyes.

You make me whole
You make me complete
My soul, my heart calls to you
Will you answer, or will I wait alone
Once I held you, once you were mine
Girl, what you do to me.

Tears stung her eyes. Damn him and his thrilling music. This was the song he'd written for her in between gigs on his first tour.

He finished the song and called up to her with a glance

toward his audience. "That song was inspired by my wife, Steph."

Everyone stared up at her. The man loved an audience.

She worked to harden her heart toward him. "Get lost, Griff."

This time he addressed her directly, looking right in her eyes. "I've never loved anyone but you."

"Awww…" Roberta and Pauline said in unison.

Something shifted in Steph's heart. She felt the truth of his words. She had loved him once. Was there still some small part of the Griff she used to know deep inside him? The man she loved before the rock 'n' roll machine ate him up and spit him out a star?

And then just like that she lost his attention. Roberta and Pauline rushed him for autographs that Griff happily signed, chatting with them amiably. He posed for some pictures with cell phone cameras.

Her heart closed against him. She'd wasted an entire year waiting for Griff to come back to her, even as the evidence mounted that she'd been abandoned. And the women he'd been with, splashed all over the tabloids, without a peep from him. No remorse, not even the decency to keep his affairs out of the press. It had devastated and embarrassed her. Finally, two years after he'd left her, she'd managed to get a new job in Clover Park, moving away from the town where everyone knew her and Griff's sordid story, to a town where no one knew her at all. She'd never mentioned him, had even gone so far as to cut her hair short to look different from before, in case any old pictures of them were circulating from the brief time when she'd been in the spotlight with him. (Once she felt comfortable, with no gossip circulating about her in town that she'd ever heard, she let her hair grow out again.) She'd started a new life for herself and refused to look back.

And now, five years later, the divorce papers finally made Griff realize he loved her. It was too late. Too damn late.

∼

The next day Dave still didn't have anything great planned for winning Steph. In desperation, last night he'd Googled "romantic things men can do" and called his sister, both of which had been less than helpful. The Internet had come up with stuff like roses, jewelry, and chocolate. But he was competing with a rock star, so he knew he had to go big. His call to Christina had been a complete disaster. As soon as she heard the name Griffin Huntley, she was like a derivative of velocity—pure annoying acceleration, going fast in one direction. Their conversation went like this:

Chris: "I want to meet him."

"No."

"Please."

"No."

"Please."

"No."

"Come on."

"No."

After several rounds of that, Chris proclaimed, "I'm not just saying this because I'm hot for the guy! I sincerely want to help you. I can distract him while you make your move on Steph."

"Look, it's not gonna happen. I wouldn't wish this guy on any woman and especially not my sister."

"I can handle myself."

"No."

They went a few more rounds before he finally threatened to hang up on her. That prompted Chris to yell, "Do something specific to Steph, not something you got off the Internet!" which was also less than helpful. What specific thing would blow Steph away? She appeared to have it all—a nice apartment, a nice job, a nice cat. What could he possibly give her?

At lunch, he took his dilemma to the teachers' lounge with his three closest women friends, all battle-worn veterans of the singles scene—Michelle (Social Studies), Courtney (French), and Julia (Language Arts). Usually he just listened to his friends chat about parents, the administration, and what was up with whatever reality TV show they were watching recently, but he was going up against a rock star. He needed the big guns, the big ammo. He needed these three.

He cleared his throat in a brief pause in the conversation over whether or not Clive should've given the pearls to Jennifer M. last night on some show he'd never heard of. "Ladies, I need your advice about..." He coughed and pulled at the collar of his button-down shirt. "Love."

Michelle, Courtney, and Julia turned to him with equal looks of shock.

Courtney shut her gaping mouth with a snap. "Is it Stephanie? Are you going to pop the question?"

The women exchanged looks of glee. He quickly filled them in on the rock-star problem.

"I don't know, Dave," Julia said in her thoughtful tone. "It sounds like a bad situation all around. Why don't you wait until she's divorced before you do anything?"

Courtney disagreed. Loudly. "She said it was over. Why should they suffer because her soon-to-be ex is an asshole?" She glared at the other two women before turning back to him with a smile. "Can I meet him? I love Twisted Star."

"Er..." he stalled.

"I know what Dave is going for here," Michelle said. She was a former cheerleader, current cheerleading coach, and very gung-ho and perky. "You want to wow her with something romantic. Am I right?"

"Awww," the women chorused.

His ears burned.

"Try a massage," Michelle said. "Women love massages. Especially a foot massage after a long day of being on your feet."

"What if he can't get her alone with Griffin hanging around?" Julia said. "I think maybe something nice like doing a chore for her. One time my boyfriend, Mike, cooked *and* washed the dishes. It was quite nice. An act of service shows love."

Courtney made a face of disgust. "Isn't that the same guy that peed in your sink when you were using the bathroom?"

"That doesn't change the act of service," Julia snapped.

"Peeing in the sink changes everything!" Courtney exclaimed.

Dave rubbed the back of his neck and wished the ladies would keep the volume down. People were starting to listen in. He didn't want everyone to know about this awkward situation he'd found himself in.

"Maybe a hike and a picnic," Michelle suggested, her eyes lighting up. "Or a long bike ride."

"Camping!" Julia exclaimed.

"A nice hotel with room service!" Courtney exclaimed.

He looked at the table. None of those things sounded quite right. "I don't know. I just don't know."

Julia put a hand on his arm. "Hey, this is Dave we're talking about. Sweet is his strong suit. He should do something sweet."

"Something an asshole rock star would never come up with," Courtney said. "Though don't tell him I said that. I would love to get his autograph or something." Her cheeks turned pink, which was very unusual for Courtney.

"I've got it!" Michelle said. "He could write her a love poem. Yes?"

"*Je serai poete et toi poesie,*" Courtney said dreamily. "It means: I'll be a poet, and you'll be poetry."

"Ladies, I'm a math teacher," he said patiently. "Poems aren't my field of expertise." He was never going to win Steph over at this rate.

"Have you heard of Fibonacci poetry?" Julia asked.

"Fibonacci?" Dave asked. "As in the numerical pattern that's often found in nature?" The Fibonacci sequence was a pattern where each number was equal to the sum of the two numbers before it—1, 1, 2, 3, 5, 8, 13, 21. The recursive sequence described spirals such as sunflowers and conch shells. He loved the Fibonacci sequence.

Julia smiled. "Exactly. We've been experimenting with it in class. You use the Fibonacci sequence to write a poem. Each line of the poem has the number of words in the sequence or you could do the number of syllables."

"I'll do the words," Dave said. "That sounds easier. Thank you. This is something Griffin will never be able to top."

The women gave him smiles that looked a little worried.

"What?" he asked.

"You'll do great, sweetie!" Michelle said.

They all nodded and smiled enthusiastically. Maybe a little too enthusiastically, but that was them. He felt good about their talk.

Griff waited outside of Steph's house after school the next day for her to get home from work. Mandy had gotten some good shots of him and Steph yesterday and last night when he sang to her, so he didn't need to stay. The thing was, now that he'd seen Steph again and met Dave, he had to hang around. The way Dave looked at Steph made Griff crazy. That was *his wife*. Sure, he hadn't been around in a few years, but facts were facts. Legally, she was his. He smiled to himself as he watched Steph pull up in her VW Beetle. He'd forgotten how feisty she was. Like a breath of fresh air after all the jaded women he'd been with in L.A.

He really did want another chance with her. And wouldn't that be even better press for him? The rocker and his hometown girl getting back together? Maybe even renewing their vows in a big splashy ceremony? Not like the first time in that dinky church she and her mother went to.

He was about to get out of the limo when Steph knocked on the window. He stepped outside.

She put her hands on her hips. "What are you doing here?"

"I wanted to see you."

"Well, I don't want to see you," she huffed.

He gave her a slow smile that melted hearts everywhere. "Can't you spare one minute to talk to your husband?"

She lifted her chin. "I don't consider you my husband. I don't even know you anymore."

He stepped closer, into her personal space. She flushed and took a quick step back.

"You remember me," he said in a low voice. "Us. We were good together." He stroked her hair and smiled, in case Mandy was still snapping pictures with her telephoto lens. Always looked good to have a smile when you were with a beautiful woman. And Steph, even after all these years, was still stunning. He wanted her just as much as he had before. The sex had always been great. That had never been a problem for them. It was just that he found it hard to be faithful when there were so many other beautiful women eager to bed the famous Griffin Huntley. It was a weakness he'd try to work on, if Steph gave him a second chance.

"If you want to talk about the divorce, I'm all ears," Steph said. "Otherwise, you should just go back to whatever seedy hotel you came from."

He held her chin. "I'm at the Four Seasons, babe."

She jerked her head away from him. "Of course you are."

She strode up the front porch steps. He followed.

She stopped, hand on the doorknob. "I swear I will call the cops if you try to force your way upstairs with me."

She was bluffing. The Steph he knew would never do anything to hurt him. She loved him.

He grinned. "What if you just invite me in?"

"What if I don't?" she said before slipping inside and shutting the door behind her.

Griff went back to the limo for a temporary retreat. Okay, so it would take some time for Steph to warm up to him again, but damn if he was going to let that geek waltz in here and steal her away. He'd wait him out. He was *not* going to lose Steph to a guy like that.

~

Dave spent an hour after school composing his first ever Fibonacci poem and thought it came out pretty good. He considered the best delivery system. In person, he could just hand it to her. Or he could slip it under her door. Or put it in the mailbox. No, to be romantic he had to go in person. Even better, he'd climb a ladder and recite the poem outside her bedroom window. Just like Rapunzel, except without the freakishly long hair.

After a brief stop to pick up some roses to go with the poem, he embarked on his quest for the fair maiden. Within minutes, he was beginning to question his Rapunzel idea. The ladder proved difficult to tie on top of his car, and he had to drive twenty-five miles per hour the whole way so it didn't fall off. But it would all be worth it, he told himself.

He pulled up in front of her place and immediately saw the limo parked out front. Damn. Griffin had gotten there first. Still, he wouldn't give up. Just another hurdle on his quest. He untied the ladder and pulled it off the top of his car. Opening the passenger-side door, he reached for the flowers on the seat. The ladder slipped a little from his grip. Too heavy. He was going to drop it. He set the ladder gently on the front lawn.

The sky was overcast, and he prayed the rain held off until he completed his task. The weather report hadn't said anything about showers. If Dave believed in signs, this would've been a bad one. But it was simply a drop in atmospheric pressure combined with the Gulf Stream. It was getting dark with all the storm clouds, and he hoped there was a light around back by her bedroom. He stuck the flowers down the front of his gray fleece jacket. Some petals came loose and fluttered to the ground.

He lifted the ladder, and the roses crushed into his throat. He shoved the flowers further down his jacket with one hand and awkwardly made his way to the back of the house with the ladder, the petals tickling his neck. He heard a car door slam behind him.

"Just ring the buzzer, man." Griffin appeared in front of him. Apparently, he'd still been in the limo. Maybe Dave would have the first chance at Steph. "You're going to slide right off the back of the house."

Dave stepped to the side, determined to stick with his

plan. "I can do this without any advice from you. I just need the right angle and some traction. It's simple physics."

Griffin rolled his eyes. "I'll ring the buzzer."

"No!"

Griffin ignored him and bounded up the front porch steps, hitting the buzzer.

"Who is it?" Steph asked.

"It's your honey," Griffin sang.

Dave dropped the ladder on the front lawn and sprinted up the porch steps. He leaned into the intercom speaker. "It's Dave."

"And Griff."

"Just Dave gets in." Steph hit the buzzer.

Dave opened the door. "You can go now," he told his nemesis.

Griffin inclined his head. "Good luck." He strolled down the steps, heading for his limo.

Dave took the stairs two at a time, secretly relieved he didn't have to actually climb the ladder. Without someone to keep it steady, it really could've slid off the back of the house. He couldn't keep up with Griffin if he was in traction.

Steph opened the door, and his mouth went dry. She wore an oversize Columbia sweatshirt with leggings.

"Columbia," he said reverently. She looked *so* sexy.

"Yup. Come on in."

She stepped back from the door, and he followed.

"I'm sorry about Griff showing up here," Steph said. She stared at his chest. He looked down, and the flowers poked his throat again.

He unzipped his jacket and pulled out the crumpled roses. Some petals stuck to his white sweater. He handed her the flowers. "For you."

She buried her nose in them. "Oh, Dave, they're beautiful. Thank you."

"Sorry they're a little squished."

"It's fine. Let me get a vase for these."

He followed her to the kitchen, his mind racing with all the romantic things he was supposed to do, because now that he was here he felt like the poem wasn't going to cut it. He really wanted to touch her. That Columbia sweatshirt made him so hot. He could give her a foot massage! Michelle had said women loved massages. And the feet were one of the top erogenous zones—another very informative Google search—without being too demanding right up front. He was sure slow and steady would get him where he needed to go with Steph. A guy like Griffin was all flash and moved like a race car. Women liked a man who took his time. That much he knew from his women friends.

While he pondered how to get her out of her pink striped fuzzy socks, he heard a tapping.

Steph turned her head toward the back of her apartment. "What was that? It sounded like it was the window."

"Probably just the blinds. I'll check on it." He made his way toward the sound, wishing it was just the blinds.

He stopped at Steph's bedroom window and pulled up the blinds. Wishing had never worked for him. He came face-to-face with Griffin standing on *his* ladder. This guy played dirty.

"What the—Griff!" Steph exclaimed from behind him. She opened the window. "What are you doing?"

Dave peered out the window. Someone in a hoodie was holding the ladder for the jerk. Griffin wasn't as dumb as he'd hoped.

Griffin went whole hog for the fairy-tale effect. "Oh, fair Steph. Roses are red—"

"Get in here! Are you crazy?" Steph grabbed his arm and tugged.

Griffin climbed in the window, looking mighty pleased with himself, and stood next to Dave. A flash of fury ran through Dave. Griffin had managed to give Steph a poem before he did on *his* ladder. It was the stupid "roses are red" poem, but still. That had been *his* plan.

Griffin went on. "Roses are red, Steph is fine—"

"You could've been killed!" Steph shouted. She gestured to Dave. "At least he was smart enough not to risk his life on a ladder."

Dave's ears burned.

Griffin hitched a thumb in his direction. "It was his idea."

Steph turned to him, eyes wide.

Dave shook his head to deny it. Then rallied to his own cause. "I planned to give you roses on a ladder like Rapunzel, and *he* convinced me not to." He jabbed a finger at Griffin. "You stole my idea! I had a poem all ready to go, and it was much better than his." He yanked it out of his pocket and handed it to Steph.

Griffin smirked at him. Dave's hands turned into fists. He'd lose in a physical altercation, he knew it, but damn, he'd love to just sock that smug look off his face.

Steph read the poem to herself and stared at it. Griffin snatched it from her fingers and read it out loud:

"Smart
Beautiful
You have
The total package
Many talents in one person."

Griffin scoffed and leered at Steph. "I'll show you a package."

"Don't talk to her like that," Dave snapped. He snatched the poem back and gave it to Steph again. "It's a Fibonacci poem. You remember the Fibonacci sequence? One, one, two, three, five..." He trailed off at her confused expression. "It's quite beautiful. Like you."

Griffin snorted.

Steph rubbed her temples. "I'm getting a headache."

"Yeah, Dave," Griffin said. "Get lost. She has a headache."

Steph narrowed her eyes at Griffin. "You go." She turned to Dave. "I'll call you later, okay?"

"Can't I stay?" Dave asked. "I planned—"

"Not now, Dave," Steph said between her teeth.

He took the hint and headed out. He should've known once Griffin showed up, Dave didn't stand a chance. He had to get to Steph first before Griffin could ruin the moment. He was halfway down the stairs when he heard Steph shout,

"Go!" and then Griffin was out the door too. Dave picked up the pace. The last thing he wanted was to spend one extra minute with that guy.

By the time he got his ladder and dragged it around to his car, the skies opened up. He dove into the car. He'd wait out the storm. Griffin's limo was still sitting there too. Dave quickly decided he wasn't leaving until that limo did. Half an hour later, the rain slowed to a drizzle, and Dave tied the ladder back on the car. The limo finally pulled away, and Dave left too, thinking about how far he was out of his league.

Sure, he'd been all macho bravado in front of Griffin, but what did he have to offer Steph that Griffin couldn't top? Griffin could buy her anything, take her on fancy vacations, drive her around in limos, take her to celebrity parties. He was probably great in the sack after sleeping with all those models. (Not that Dave liked to think about that.) Dave had only slept with seven women. None of them had complained about him in bed, but they hadn't sung his praises either.

In retrospect, he should've had his past sexual partners fill out a survey afterwards, rating different aspects of his love-making on a scale of 1 to 5. Those kind of data points would've helped him improve exponentially, making his present situation much easier to deal with confidently. How could he possibly compare to a player like Griffin?

Why in the world had Steph ever given Dave a second look? He wasn't ugly, he knew that. And he kept in shape. Still, he'd been told, on more than one occasion, he resembled the mild-mannered Clark Kent. It was the glasses and dark brown hair, he was sure. Now, he was in some bizarro world going up against what his women friends would call a mimbo —a male bimbo. A very famous one. Not exactly an even playing field there.

He impulsively stopped at The Dancing Cow on his way home in hopes that a giant bowl of sugar would somehow help him figure out just how the hell he was supposed to compete with a freaking rock star. The shop was empty. He checked the clock on the wall. It was nearly six thirty. He figured most people were home eating dinner, not stuffing themselves with junk.

Barry was working the register. They'd met last weekend when Dave went to Barry and Amber's wedding as Steph's date.

"Hi, Barry."

"Good evening," Barry replied cheerfully. "Oh, hey, I remember you from the wedding. You're Steph's boyfriend, Dave."

Dave inclined his head. He didn't know if that was true anymore. He crossed to the counter with the bowls and took an extra-large.

"Ten percent off for friends," Barry called.

"Thanks."

Dave filled the bowl with chocolate peanut butter fro-yo, then headed to the candy bar, where he scooped on crumbled Oreo cookies, chocolate chips, Gummi bears, Heath bar, and mini-Reese's peanut-butter cups. He shifted down the counter to pump three huge globs of hot fudge over the whole thing. Finally, he set it on the scale to pay.

"Someone's in the mood for chocolate," Barry said with a huge, friendly smile.

"Yup," Dave said. "I thought you'd be on a honeymoon."

"We took the long weekend in Cape May, but Amber didn't want to leave her classroom for too long. We'll take the real honeymoon over winter break." Barry rang him up. "Aruba."

Dave nodded absentmindedly. He paid a ridiculous amount, even with ten percent off, and took a seat at a long counter by the window. He took the first spoonful, but his throat was tight, and he set the spoon down. He dropped his head in his hands and stared at the table.

"Hey, you okay?"

Dave raised a hand. "Fine." He heaved a sigh and was about to leave when Barry took the seat right next to him.

A beat passed while Dave sat uncomfortably, staring out the window, unsure why Barry was sitting there. They weren't exactly friends. He'd only met him briefly at the wedding. He could feel the other man's stare.

Finally Dave turned. "What?"

Barry shook his head. "Nothing. What's got you so depressed that you can't even eat that delicious pile of sugar?" He indicated the mess of candy sitting untouched.

Dave said nothing.

"Putting two and two together," Barry said, "a giant bowl of candy and looking depressed, I'd say woman troubles."

Dave grunted and stared at the table. He really didn't want to talk about this with another guy. It was a blow to the ego to have a famous rock star top you in the man department. Women thought his dilemma romantic—how to win the girl. Men would see it for what it was—a ballbuster.

"Steph's crazy about you," Barry said.

Dave turned in surprise.

Barry nodded. "I know this for a fact because she's good friends with my wife, Amber. Marriage confidentiality rules." He nodded sagely. "My wife—I just love saying that—*my wife*. Anyway, we tell each other everything anyone tells us, but it stops right there"—he circled his hand—"in the circle of marriage confidentiality."

"Steph's married," Dave muttered.

"I heard," Barry said sympathetically.

Dave stood and grabbed the bowl of uneaten fro-yo. "See you around."

"Wait, don't go. I'm sure I can help you. I know Steph. I've got the inside scoop between her and Amber."

Dave shook his head. "You can't help me. Not unless you can turn me into a rock star."

Barry's eyes lit up. "Stay right there."

A few minutes later, over Dave's protests, Barry was putting the necessary items into the trunk of Dave's car.

"I'm not doing this," Dave said.

Barry patted his arm. "Just in case," he said with a wink.

5

Griff finished his room service dinner in his briefs while watching the home channel that always had those happy families moving into their new homes. He liked to pretend sometimes that he was part of one of those families, nestled in their new home, loving just being together. Life on the road wasn't as glamorous as it first seemed—hotels blended together, lots of solitary meals, living out of a suitcase.

He thought again of Steph. She was still keeping him at a distance. If he could just get through that anger, he thought they could connect again. She was still the same person. He'd changed, sure, but he knew he was a better man when he was with her than he ever was on his own. On impulse, he called his manager, Bill.

"I need another week," he said. "Cancel *The Bridgette Show.*"

"You can't cancel three days before!" Bill hollered. "Do you have any idea how many strings I had to pull to get you that gig?"

Griff held the phone away from his ear while Bill worked his way through a furious tirade. When he'd wound down, Griff said, "Look, I'm going to get press without that show." *And my wife back,* he added silently.

Bill switched to a cajoling tone that Griff tuned out. The

truth was, he'd been in a slump musically speaking. Steph had been his muse for all of his biggest hits. He set the phone down as the inklings of a melody tickled his brain. He grabbed his guitar to capture that gift. He hadn't written an original song in a year. He composed like a madman for the rest of the night, adding lyrics for the song inspired by Steph. He called it "Missing Limb."

He played the finished song, euphoric in his creation. This was what it was all about—the music. It was powerful stuff. He let out a satisfied sigh as he carefully tucked the guitar back in its case.

Whether Steph wanted him around or not, he needed to be near her. She was his muse.

~

That night, Dave went from worried to depressed during his phone call with Steph.

"Dave," she said. "I'm so sorry about this mess with Griff. I don't want you in the middle of it. He leaves on Saturday, so let's just wait to see each other until he's gone, okay? Hopefully we can put all this behind us."

He didn't agree to wait until Saturday. He couldn't afford to give Griffin three whole days to win Steph over while he sat back and did nothing. So he told her the truth, minus one small part, because it was time to bring out the big guns no matter how ridiculous.

"I'll be glad to put this behind us too," he said.

"Good." She sounded relieved. "I'll call you Saturday. Thanks for understanding. Bye."

He hung up and promptly went to his car to unload the stuff Barry had put in there. This was a good strategic move, better than anything he'd come up with so far if Barry's enthusiasm was any indication. This was the big time—the battle of his life, no rules, all-out till the end. It would all be worth it to win Steph.

~

After no small amount of convincing on Jaz's part, Steph agreed to meet her friend for drinks at Garner's the next night. They sat at the bar sipping martinis and chatting.

"Am I too late?" Amber asked, a little out of breath as she rushed up to them. She scanned the restaurant and turned to Steph, her eyes wide. "I got here as soon as I heard. I was asleep last night when Bare got home, or I would've heard earlier. And then this morning…" A flush crept up her neck. "Anyway, I just heard. Bare can go a little overboard. I try to pull him back when I can." She scanned the restaurant again and halted, staring at the back of the restaurant. "I'm so sorry—"

"Oh, boy," Jaz said. "I thought it was just a romantic dinner."

Steph's stomach pitched. What now? She looked to where her friends were staring and reached for calm. "I told him I needed some time. I specifically said Saturday."

Jaz giggled. "I think it's sweet."

Steph sent Jaz a dark look. "I can't believe you went behind my back."

Jaz held her hands up. "I'm sorry. He stopped by the studio, and he was just so earnest. He loves you, Steph. That can't be bad."

"Sorry," Amber said meekly. "You're going to get the Bare treatment, except Bare never mentioned…" She giggled and turned to Jaz. The two of them cracked up.

Steph shook her head, crossed to the dining area, and stared. Dave was standing next to a karaoke machine, a microphone set up in front of him, wearing a green Shrek T-shirt. And ogre ears. The man owned ogre ears?

Omigod. He had a ukulele.

His face lit up when he saw her. Some of the regulars turned to smile at her to see how she was taking it.

She forced a smile as she approached Dave. Jaz and Amber stayed behind at the bar. Or maybe they left. She wished she could too.

"What are you doing?" she ground out.

He hit a button and the music blasted out. Dave launched

into an enthusiastic rendition of Smashmouth's "I'm a Believer" from *Shrek*.

He belted out the lyrics while strumming the ukulele. The clash of notes was jarring.

She backed up. The next line of the song rang out too close to the mike, and a screeching feedback rang through the room. Dave kept going, the ogre ears bouncing in time.

Steph sank into a chair and simply gawked. He was terrible. Completely off-key. He windmilled one arm before a dramatic ukulele strum and danced what could best be described as jumping jacks. Combined with the green shirt and ears, a vision of a leprechaun came to mind. A hysterical laugh bubbled up inside her.

The ogre ears tipped precariously forward, jutting out like horns over his glasses. He kept singing.

She bit her lip. *Don't laugh. He's really trying.* Heat crept up her neck as more people wandered over from the bar to watch. *Why, Dave? Why? And, Barry, I'm going to kill you.*

Dave could feel the crowd getting behind him now, clapping in time to the music. He shoved the ogre ears back in place. He couldn't read Steph's expression from here, but he had to keep going. This song was meant to say what was in his heart. And if he wanted to stand a chance against Griffin, he had to go big. He could rock 'n' roll too. The karaoke had been Barry's idea, but when Dave had found his favorite song from the *Shrek* soundtrack on the playlist, he knew he had to go all out in costume. Plus he already had the ogre ears, T-shirt, and ukulele.

He put the ukulele down so he could really move. The swim! He held his nose and wiggled down in a dive. He knew all the old dances from his grandmother. Finally it came in handy!

He leaped up and pounded his heart, pointing to Steph. *Yes, I do believe. In us!*

She slid further down in her chair.

The mashed potato! "I love you, Steph!"

He lost the beat as his eyes locked with a woman who appeared to be glaring at him. Was that his sister? He'd mentioned his plan to wow Steph at Garner's, but he never imagined Christina would take the hour-plus train ride out from Brooklyn to see it. He tried to jump back in with the lyrics. Something was off. The song blared on. He bounced up and down a few times, stuttering over the words. The clapping trailed off.

He grabbed the ukulele. Mad strumming! Finally he recognized the chorus again. *I'm cooking now!*

Run and slide on his knees! The other way! Would this song never end? Sweat ran down his face. He wasn't sure if Steph was getting his message.

Jump up and down. He returned to the mike. "Yeah, yeah, yeah!" Dave gave it his all.

The mike screeched, and he pulled it off the stand, leaving the ukulele behind as he recognized the last notes. Big finish. Run and slide on his knees right to Steph's feet. "I believe in us," he told her in a husky voice.

A few people clapped. "Thank you," he said in the mike.

Steph grabbed his arm and stared. "Did you get a tattoo?"

The mike picked up her voice, and it rang out through the restaurant. A few people giggled. He shut off the mike. His ears burned as he glanced down at the heart now emblazoned on his bicep. It was a dumb idea. He could never pull off a badass tattoo.

"One of my students does fake tattoos," he admitted. "It was supposed to be symbolic. I'm wearing my heart on my sleeve like Shrek does for Fiona."

At Steph's horrified expression, he added, "Except you're more like the princess version of Fiona than the ogre version."

Her eyebrows scrunched together. He wasn't sure if she thought he was crazy or if she didn't believe his sincerity. He reached for another way to convince her of his intentions. "Steph, together we could be a prime number, indivisible except only by ourselves, though I don't think that would happen. I think we have a future—"

"Begging, Dave?" drawled a voice from behind Steph.

Dave rose to his full height to stare down his nemesis.

"Nice ears." Griffin snatched the mike from Dave's hands and approached the karaoke machine. He turned it off and addressed his audience. "This song is very special to me."

Someone in the audience screamed, "Aaaah! It's Griffin Huntley! I love you, Griffin!"

Everyone was going crazy, screaming and clapping. Especially the women. Griffin raised a hand. "Thank you, thank you." When they finally quieted, he continued, "I wrote this song for my wife, Steph. Honey, this one's for you."

Flashes went off as people took pictures of the famous Griffin Huntley giving an impromptu concert. Dave watched Steph carefully for her reaction. She was riveted, just like the rest of them. His heart sank.

Steph stared as Griff sang without music to a rapt audience. It was the song that had made him famous. The song that he'd written for her the day after her mother had died. The song that had come to him, he said, because of his love for her. "All for You" was an anthem that built, starting slow and building to a rocking chorus. In the cozy confines of the restaurant, his voice was beautiful, rolling with the gorgeous melody. There was a reason she never listened to his music. It reached past her defenses and wrapped around her heart.

She could feel Dave staring at her, but like everyone else she was mesmerized by the music, his voice, his charismatic presence. Griffin Huntley was made to be a rock star.

Tears welled up in her eyes as the memories came flooding back. Even though she'd known her mom would die soon, the day she did finally pass, quietly in her sleep, was still a shock. Steph had sat with her just the night before, holding her hand as she rested in the hospital bed they'd moved into her home. Griff had been with them too for a while, until her mom asked him to take Joey out for ice cream. Her mom had talked to her about the future. She wanted to hear all the things that Steph had planned for her life, all her dreams. And Steph, somehow knowing deep down that it was near the end, had told her mom everything she hoped for in her life with Griff. How she hoped he would make it big, how they would have children and bring them up with music too, how they'd travel the world as a family, how they'd make sure they did some good in the world.

Her mom had smiled and squeezed her hand. "I like that." She drew in a raspy breath. "Remember you, Steph." Another raspy breath. Then so quiet, she almost missed it, she said, "Your dreams too."

Steph hadn't understood at the time. Her dreams were Griff's dreams; they were one and the same. When she'd explained that, her mom had looked into her eyes, hers burning with intent. "You. Don't forget…you."

Then she'd fallen asleep, never to wake again.

"Steph, are you okay?"

She turned toward the voice, still lost in the memories. She blinked at the incongruous vision before her. Dave, the ogre ears still on his head, as her husband's voice reached out to her through the power of music, reminding her of the love they once had, reminding her of the loss of her mother.

She jumped up so fast her chair knocked over. She turned and ran. Straight out of the restaurant. Down the sidewalk. No destination in mind, just needing some space to cry in peace. She'd thought she'd put her time with Griff behind her, but now here he was, messing with her head, reminding her of all that she'd lost back then. Footsteps pounded behind her. Had to be Dave. Griff would never leave his audience mid-song.

She stopped and turned to face the man she loved, who was now trying to be just like the man she no longer loved. She wanted the old Dave back. A tear leaked out.

"Don't cry," he said, drawing her in close for a hug.

She looked over his shoulder. "I'll cry if I damn well feel like it."

He pulled back to look in her eyes. His head cocked to the

side and the ogre ears bobbled. "Is it Griffin you're crying about?"

She snatched the ogre ears off his head. It was hard to take him seriously like that. "It's that stupid song."

"Oh. What about it?"

"He wrote it right after my mom died." The tears came in earnest. "I miss her so much."

He held her and stroked her hair while she sobbed into his shirt. A few moments later, she took a shaky breath. She looked up at his concerned face and took a chance, telling him the other part of why she was upset. "His songs remind me of when we were together. And it hurts because he abandoned me and cheated on me, and I hate that I feel anything about him at all!"

"He never deserved you. Don't listen to his songs anymore."

She pulled away. "And you! Stop trying to one-up Griff. He sings a song, you sing a song. He has a tattoo, you get a tattoo. I just want you to be yourself. It's not a competition, and I'm not some prize to fight over."

He wiped away a tear with the pad of his thumb. "That's where you're wrong. You are a prize, and I will fight for you."

"I want the old Dave back. Just ignore Griff. He's leaving the day after tomorrow."

"Good. But I am the same person. I didn't sing you that song because Griffin's a rock star. I sang it so you'd know how I feel." At her silence, he added, "It was Barry's idea."

She wiped her eyes, realizing that he couldn't have known that Griff had serenaded her the other night. "What about the tattoo?"

He smiled sheepishly. "Impulse decision. I liked the metaphor."

Griff jogged up to them. "Hey, you didn't hear the end of the song. They're shouting encore. My driver's dropping off my guitar. Steph, come back inside and listen. I have a new song I really want you to hear. I wrote it last night. You're my muse, babe."

"I'm sure you can manage without me," Steph said. His

claim that she was his muse was short-lived once the record company brought in their people.

Griff looked surprised that anyone would want to miss him performing new material. He recovered in a snap and turned to Dave. "Nice ogre act, geek."

"Not everyone can be a brainless rock star," Dave snapped.

Griff rushed at Dave, fisting his Shrek T-shirt in one hand. "I got a degree in real life while you were cozied up with your calculator."

"I have to warn you," Dave said, squinting his eyes like a tough guy, even though Griff still had him by the shirt. "I've defeated the *Street Fighter* video game in two hours twenty-three minutes."

"Ooh, I'm real—" Griff's sarcastic reply was cut off when a petite woman came charging out of the restaurant and launched herself on Griff's back, nearly knocking both men over. Griff dropped his hold on Dave and grabbed the arms of the woman who was about to choke off his oxygen supply.

"Chris!" Dave exclaimed.

Steph turned to Dave with wide eyes. "You know her?"

Griff managed to get the crazed woman off his back and twisted around to pin her wrists in one hand. "Who the hell are you?"

The woman smiled demurely at complete odds with her uber-calm, uber-threatening voice. "I'm Christina Olsen, and you messed with the wrong guy."

Dave cleared his throat. "Stephanie, meet my sister, Christina."

Christina smiled sweetly. "Hi, Stephanie, nice to meet you finally. I've heard a lot about you. All good things. I'd shake your hand, but I'm a little tied up."

Griff released her wrists and took a step closer to Steph. Christina wasn't happy with that move. She did a head swivel that Steph wished she could pull off before going toe-to-toe with Griff.

"Okay, we all know who you are," Christina said, jabbing

her finger in Griff's chest. She lowered her voice dramatically "The great Griffin Huntley." More finger jabs followed that had Griff backing up as Christina continued. "Don't get me wrong." *Jab.* "I'm your number one fan." *Jab.* "But you crossed a line here with Stephanie." *Jab.* Griff's back was against the wall, and Christina was right up against his front. "She asked you for a divorce, very nicely I hear. She's in love with my brother, who's in love with her back, so I ask you"—she paused and took them all in—"who doesn't belong in this picture?"

"Chris, I don't need you to—" Dave started.

"I'll tell you who doesn't belong in this picture," Griff snarled. "You and your brother. Steph was my wife first."

Steph backed away from the pair and stood by Dave's side, who promptly wrapped his arm around her.

Christina and Griff stared each other down. People started coming out of the restaurant, probably wondering where Griff had gone after promising more music.

"Oh, look," Christina said with a big smile. "Your favorite. We have an audience."

Then she threw her arms around Griff's neck and kissed him for all she was worth. Steph turned to Dave for his reaction to this strange turn of events when he shocked the hell out of her by gripping her hair in one hand as his mouth crashed down over hers. His other arm wrapped around her waist, pressing her flush against his body. The kiss was hard, raw, and unbelievably erotic as his tongue thrust inside. She could do nothing but cling to him as he ravaged her mouth, lost in the unexpected feverish kiss.

Griff staggered back as Christina finally let him up for air.

"Told you," Christina said to Griff with a smirk. She inclined her head to where Dave was still kissing Steph like a sex-starved man. He probably was. Griff couldn't imagine a guy like Dave saw a lot of action. So why did he have to go after the one woman Griff couldn't let go?

Griff set the crazy woman away from him. He scanned the crowd and quickly found Mandy in her usual hoodie.

He headed in her direction when Christina pulled on his arm. "What?" he snapped.

She gave him a withering look. The woman had balls, he'd give her that much. Most women were all smiles and soft words around him.

She leaned up on tiptoe to whisper in his ear and, in that terrifying moment between when her mouth reached his ear and when she finally spoke, he thought she might just bite his ear off.

"If you touch a hair on Dave's head," she whispered, "I will castrate you."

He straightened, relieved to still have his ear. "Message received."

Mandy was taking pictures of him and this lunatic now. He had to stop her. He was about to leave when Christina pulled on his arm again.

He turned back to her. "I get it!"

She smiled up at him under her lashes and pressed a card into his hand. "Call me if you ever want to be with a real woman. Ya know, instead of a plastic doll."

He pointed at her. "You're crazy."

"Only when called upon," she said with a wink.

She didn't leave, just stood there studying him, making him feel uncomfortable. He turned away. "Mandy, wait up!"

Mandy was moving at a pretty good pace down the sidewalk, heading toward her rental car. That was not good. She usually would talk to him. He broke into a run and caught up with her at her car.

"You can't use those pictures," he said. "Please. It looks really bad for me to be kissing one woman in front of my wife, let alone me watching my wife kiss another man."

"It doesn't matter what I do, Griff," she said in her throaty smoker's voice. She pushed the hood off her head. She'd dyed her hair. Griff stared. Her blond hair was now dark brown and straightened. And long. It looked a lot like Steph's hair, actually.

"Did you get a wig?" he couldn't help but ask. He didn't remember her hair being that long.

"A lot of people got those shots and video," she huffed. "That stuff's already online now. My contribution only means I get to keep my job."

"I'll get you better shots soon," he said. "I promise. You gotta help me out. Gotta make me look good. I need this."

She unlocked her car and slid in, powering down the window. "I go where you go, but you have to put in a little effort. The camera doesn't lie."

"I know, I know. I will. Promise."

Mandy gave him a small smile, one corner of her mouth quirking up. "Don't worry about her, Griff. I still love you."

He gave her his slow, sexy smile in appreciation of her always having his back. He'd never slept with her because that usually ended badly, and he couldn't afford to have Mandy mad at him. She could do some serious damage to him in the press.

"Thanks, Mandy, you're the best."

"Remember that," she said before she drove away.

—————

6

"I'm just saying, I wouldn't kick Griffin Huntley out of bed." Jaz waggled her eyebrows.

"Me either," Amber chimed in.

Steph was with her friends at Amber's house for a sorely needed girls' night in on Friday night. They were eating Thai food in the living room.

Amber's husband, Bare, popped his head out of the kitchen and peered at them. "What's this now?"

"Girl talk," Amber quickly said.

"Amber," he growled and went back to the kitchen.

Amber's face flushed. She leaped up from the sofa. "I'll be right back, guys."

It was really quiet in the kitchen, so Steph whispered her confession to Jaz. "I haven't even gotten Dave into bed. Every time I see Dave, Griff shows up."

Jaz's eyes widened. "Is Griff stalking you?"

Goose bumps ran down Steph's arms at the thought. It was strange the way Griff kept popping up. She hadn't told him where she'd be any of those times.

She ate some more pad Thai, considering. "Maybe he is," she finally said.

Jaz leaned forward across the coffee table. "Would he hurt you?"

"No, never," Steph replied immediately. Not the Griff she knew. They'd only dated six months before their three months of marriage, but he'd been open with her, even vulnerable at times, as he shared his sometimes painful memories of childhood with her. And he was so good with Joey. He wasn't a violent man. At least not until he'd gotten a look at Dave. Of course, Dave hadn't seemed like the type to get into a physical altercation before he met Griff either. It was like some kind of manly pissing contest. Ridiculous.

Steph went back to her meal.

Jaz chewed her basil chicken before saying, "Still, it's creepy."

Steph waved that away. "He's leaving tomorrow, so I don't have to worry."

"You can call Chief O'Hare if you feel unsafe," Jaz said. "You know he'll take that seriously."

"I know." Especially since Steph was friends with Ryan O'Hare's wife, Liz. They both worked at Clover Park Elementary.

They went back to eating in comfortable silence. A few minutes later, Steph glanced at Amber's food sitting untouched. "Amber?" she called.

"Coming!" Amber gasped.

Jaz and Steph exchanged an astonished look. *Omigod*, Jaz mouthed.

I know, Steph mouthed back.

"Should we go?" Jaz whispered.

They stared at each other, then burst into laughter, covering their mouths to smother the noise. Jaz got up and tiptoed toward the kitchen.

"Don't!" Steph hissed.

Jaz stopped and did a little thrusting move. "Oh, Bar-ry," she whispered.

"Shh-shh-shh," Steph whispered, giggling.

They went back to eating. Jaz kept holding a hand to her ear like she was listening for the big finish.

Amber finally returned, smoothing her hair. "So, what'd I miss? Bare needed help with something in the kitchen."

"Something," Jaz quipped.

Amber returned to her lemongrass chicken. "Mmm…something."

Jaz filled her in. "We think Griff might be stalking Steph, but she's not worried, and he's leaving tomorrow. Have you met him?"

"Yeah," Amber said. "He was at the school." She bit her lip, eyes dancing mischievously, and said louder, "He's even better looking in person."

Bare popped his head back in. "Amber," he growled.

Amber flushed, but stayed where she was.

Bare returned to the kitchen.

Amber giggled. "I'll pay for that later," she whispered in a delighted tone. She turned to Steph. "You want to stay here tonight so you don't have to worry about Griff? We've got a guest room."

"As much as I'd love to hear you and Bare going at it"—Steph raised her voice for Bare's benefit—"all night long, I'll pass."

"You can stay with me," Jaz offered.

"That's okay," Steph said. "I'll be fine."

After dinner, they drank wine and watched this insane *Zombie Bonanza* show Amber was obsessed with. Jaz kept throwing popcorn at the screen every time a victim innocently went to check out a strange noise. Steph relaxed for the first time since Griff had showed up in town. She couldn't wait for him to go back to L.A. Things would get back on track with Dave. If that kiss outside Garner's was any indication, Dave had a raw, carnal side to him she was very willing to explore.

Later that night, Bare insisted on driving Steph and Jaz home, even though it was just a few blocks' walk in the dark. She waved goodbye to her friends, checked the dark street for a limo, and finding none, let herself in the house with no worries. Not that she could see all that much. There was only one streetlight, but a limo would've stuck out, she was sure.

She climbed the stairs, opened her front door, turned on the light, and froze.

Something was off. Her lamp was knocked over, and the fake oranges in the decorative bowl were scattered all over the floor. Her evil cat, Loki, was perched on top of the sofa, hissing at something on the other side, out of sight.

Heart racing, Steph thought of all those innocent, stupid people she'd just watched on *Zombie Bonanza* that walked straight into the zombies' clutches. She grabbed the lamp as a weapon and slowly crossed to where Loki was staring. Something furry and gray scurried past, running right over her foot. "Ahhh!"

Loki jumped off the sofa and raced to the bedroom.

Holy shit. Was that a mouse or a rat? It looked huge. Steph shuddered. She set the lamp back on the end table and tiptoed to the kitchen, where the mouse-rat had been heading. That would explain the mess if Loki had been chasing it around her apartment. The beast was huddled behind Loki's food dish.

The beady black eyes stared at her. It smelled her fear. The whiskers twitched, revealing sharp little teeth. It was a largish mouse, she was pretty sure, not a rat. She searched for something to catch it with. She couldn't sleep tonight knowing a mouse was loose in her apartment. What if it burrowed in her hair? Or stuck its little mouse head in her mouth when she was sleeping? Or tried to eat her eyeball?

"Don't move," she told it. "I'm getting a nice comfy box for you."

She slowly backed away so as not to provoke it and went to her bedroom in search of a shoebox.

She peered under her bed, where the cat was huddled. "Loki, get your ass out here and earn your keep."

She reached for Loki, who swiped at her. His claws caught her hand. "Ow! You're a disgrace to cats everywhere. I can't believe you only hunt my hair clips. This is what you were made for!"

She held her hand. It stung so bad. A few drops of blood appeared. Great. Now the giant mouse would smell blood and try to devour her, one sharp little bite at a time, in her sleep. She opened her closet and pulled a shoebox off the top shelf, leaving the shoes behind. She returned to the kitchen with the shoebox. No mouse.

"Come out, come out, wherever you are," she called. "I've got a nice comfy new house for you."

She looked all around the kitchen, opened all the cabinets, and peered behind the appliances. She wandered out to the living room. "Ah!" she yelped.

It was on the sofa! She ran toward it, box open, and it zipped across the sofa and disappeared into her bedroom. She halted. She'd never sleep again. Loki came tearing out of there and huddled in the corner of the living room. She slammed the bedroom door.

She'd have to move, that was all. If that beast was sitting on her pillow, she could never sleep on it again. She grabbed the blanket from the sofa and covered the crack under the bedroom door. At least now it was contained. But what if it pooped on her bed? She'd have to burn the sheets.

She ripped back the blanket and flung open the door. She checked all over the bedroom. "Here, mousie." She stomped her feet to get it moving and was about to give up when a flash of gray zipped out the door. Loki hissed. She ran to the living room. No mouse. Loki was on top of the sofa, his eyes so wide the whites were showing.

"You are so fired," she told Loki. And because there was no way she could sit down or do anything until that mouse was out of her house, she called Dave.

"Are you busy?" she asked. She could hear guy voices in the background.

"Nah."

"What are you doing?"

"Nothing."

"Sure?"

"It's just Pokémon night with the guys."

"Poker?" Sometimes his Brooklyn accent showed itself on certain words. He dropped his Rs when she least expected it.

"No, Pok-e-mon." He enunciated each syllable clearly.

Wasn't that the trading card game some of the younger kids played at recess? Adults played that too? Before she could ask, the mouse raced along the wall and headed behind her refrigerator. What if it got inside the refrigerator? What if she opened her pasta salad and found a dead mouse in there?

"There's a giant rat!" she exclaimed. "Can you come over?"

"I'll be right over," Dave said. "Don't worry. I've had a lot of experience with rats in Brooklyn."

"Bless you."

A short while later, Dave arrived, her hero. She hugged him. "It's in the kitchen."

"Where's your broom?" he asked.

"In the closet in the kitchen. Can you get it? I don't want to go in there."

He nodded once and got the broom. He wielded it like a weapon.

"What are you going to do?" she asked from a safe distance.

"I'm going to kill it."

"You can't kill it! Just get it out of here."

"These things spread diseases. Believe me, you want it gone."

"It might be a mouse," she said. "Actually, I'm sure it's a mouse. I know I said it was a rat because it's huge, but it just seems huge because it's touching my stuff." A flash of gray went past. "There it is!"

Dave took off, swiping at the mouse, which led him on a merry chase around the apartment. Loki watched from a safe distance, looking terrified.

Steph got on the sofa and pulled her legs up so the mouse wouldn't accidentally run over her foot again. Dave trapped it by the sofa when it ran underneath.

Steph jumped up. "Ah! Dave!" she screamed.

Someone pounded on the door. "Steph! Are you okay?"

Griff?

"Dave!" she hollered again. The mouse had reappeared on the other side of the sofa.

Dave came flying toward her, and the broom bumped into her calf with a whack.

"Ow!" Steph cried.

"Steph! Let me in!" Griff hollered. "I'll break this door down." A hard thump sounded on the front door.

"Dave!" she screamed, pointing to where the mouse was now hovering by the wall.

The front door thumped again. Steph tore her gaze from the mouse. Another thump. The wooden door actually bulged. *Shit*. He really was going to break the door down. Steph ran to the front door and flung it open. Griff came tumbling in just as Dave ran by with the broom after the mouse that was heading for her bedroom again.

"Get it!" she screamed. "Don't let it touch my bed!"

"What is going on here?" Griff asked. "I thought you were in trouble."

Steph spared him a quick glance while she gathered all the oranges off the floor before Dave killed himself on them. "Dave's trying to catch the mouse that just ran into my bedroom!"

Griff nodded. "I got this."

He left. She could hear Dave banging around in her bedroom as the broom thwacked the floor and walls. The mouse tore out of there. She jumped back on the sofa to find Loki trembling in fear. She scooped up the cat and stroked his quivering body. "You are the worst hunter ever, Loki."

Loki made no reply.

Griff returned with a baseball bat.

"Omigod, Griff, what are you doing?" Steph asked. "Where did you get that?"

"Your neighbor. I'm going to get the mouse."

She watched in horror as both Dave and Griff chased the mouse around the apartment, wooden bat and broom swinging wildly. Dave swung the broom down just as Griff swung the bat, nearly taking out Dave's ankle.

"Guys, stop!" Steph exclaimed. "You can't both hunt the mouse. You're going to hurt each other."

"I'll do it," Dave said. His eyes never left his prey.

"I got it, honey," Griff said, charging toward her bedroom.

She heard a scuffle, several thumps, and a whack as the bat hit wood. "Don't destroy my furniture, Griff!"

Suddenly a flash of gray zipped close by her feet, which was enough to prompt Loki to leap out of her arms and run in the opposite direction. The cat ran toward the bedroom just as Dave and Griff tried to get through the doorway at the same time. The cat tripped Griff, who knocked into Dave, and they both went face first to the floor.

She looked wildly around for the mouse and saw it heading down the apartment hallway just outside of her front door that Griff had forgotten to close. She leaped for the front door, slammed it closed, and blocked the crack with the blanket.

"It's gone!" she declared.

"Get off me," Dave said.

Griff and Dave untangled from each other and stood.

Steph took a deep, calming breath. "That was exciting."

She took the bat and broom from the two men. "Thanks for helping," she said. She peered behind them into her bedroom. There was a splinter in the post of the footboard.

"Griff, you ruined my bed frame," she said.

"That's why a broom is better," Dave said.

"I'll buy you a new one," Griff said.

"What are you doing here?" she asked Griff.

He looked uneasy for a moment, but quickly recovered. "I made us reservations for lunch at Grinaldi's in the city tomorrow. I stopped by to see if you'd go. For old times' sake. I got us a table with an amazing skyline view."

Grinaldi's was one of the top restaurants in the city, and the place to see and be seen. Celebrities flocked to the restaurant that took up the top floor of the Metro Six building. Still, Steph was suspicious. He could've called for that invitation. He had to have been camped out close by.

She shook her head.

Dave piped up. "Old times are dead and gone."

Griff's head whipped around. "I deserve at least one meal with *my wife*. We have things to talk about."

"Then you should've called her at least once in the last five years," Dave said.

The two men glared at each other. The testosterone level rose in the room.

"Everyone calm down," Steph said. "Griff, no, but thanks. I have plans with Dave." She didn't, but he didn't know that.

"She's got plans with me," Dave immediately agreed.

"Have a good trip tomorrow," Steph said to Griff. "Be a stranger, would ya?"

Griff turned to Dave with a murderous look. "What kind of plans?"

The corner of Dave's mouth lifted. "Wouldn't you like to know?"

Griff got in Dave's face. "I have a right to know. A husband's right."

Dave didn't back down. "You have zero rights," he barked. "Less than zero. Zilch."

"I'm not leaving until Steph and I talk," Griff snarled.

"Oh, you're leaving all right," Dave said, grabbing Griff's arm and escorting him to the door. Griff shook him off and shoved him hard. Dave stumbled backward.

"Griff, stop!" Steph said. "No fighting."

Dave rushed forward and shoved Griff, who stumbled back into the door. Steph's eyes widened.

"I said no fighting!" she hollered.

The two men circled each other. Dave held both fists up like a boxer and started bobbing and weaving. Steph groaned. This could not end well.

"Both of you out," she said. "If you're going to beat up on each other, I don't want to see it." She grabbed both their arms and pushed them out the door.

"But, Steph," Dave said.

"Come on," Griff said.

"Out," she said before she shut the door and locked it. She sank against the door, exhausted. She hoped they would calm down without her as a witness. She figured it was their pride and ego they were trying to preserve in front of her.

She really did not need to see Dave get his ass kicked.

Dave stood on the sidewalk for a moment, unsure if he should go back for Steph or give her some space. He'd only gone to Pokémon night because Steph was going to girls' night. Also, he figured he could ask the guys what they thought his next move should be. He had zero ideas. How could he? He'd never had to compete with a famous rock star before. Unfortunately, his guy friends had even less of a clue than he had with women. Frank had suggested inviting her to Pokémon night, but Dave suspected that was because Frank wanted a beautiful woman there. He'd been single for a couple of years now and would likely hit on Steph. Andy had suggested giving her a puppy, but she already had a cat. Kyle suggested Dave cook her dinner and had even given him *The Player's Guide to Eating In* from his own bookshelf. Except Dave couldn't cook. He usually got four orders of chicken with mixed vegetables from Sunny Garden and ate that all week. The mouse had been the perfect excuse to both look like a hero to Steph and hang out with her. Until Griffin arrived.

"Hey, you want to get a beer?" Griffin called.

Dave's jaw dropped. Griffin slouched against the limo, hands in his pockets.

"With you?" Dave asked.

"Yeah, we'll work things out. Easier over a beer, don't you think?"

Dave was suspicious, but he'd do just about anything to get things back on track with Steph. "All right."

They walked the few blocks to Garner's bar in silence. Griffin claimed a couple of seats at the bar. Soon a crowd had gathered, all women, fawning over Griffin. The guy didn't invent anything great like nanotechnology or even rock 'n' roll. Griffin signed autographs and took some pictures with the locals.

Dave nursed a beer, ready to bail on this whole working-things-out idea. Only his love for Steph kept him glued to the barstool next to the puffed-up singer. A long, boring time later, Griffin finally remembered Dave.

"That's all for now, folks," Griffin said. "I'm here to catch up with my old pal Dave."

The crowd reluctantly dispersed. A beautiful redhead gave Griffin a napkin with her number while she leaned in close and whispered something in his ear. Griffin grinned, tucked the napkin in his pocket, and gave her a little wave goodbye.

"Nice," Dave muttered under his breath. Real husband material. The guy definitely didn't deserve Steph.

Griffin eyed Dave. "So, tell me about you, Dave."

Dave was taken aback. "What do you want to know?"

Griffin took a pull on his beer. "What does Steph see in you?"

He considered the question. "I'm a nice guy. Women like that."

Griffin raised a skeptical brow. "Yeah? No offense, but you seem like a bit of a wimp to me."

"No offense, but you seem like a bit of an asshole to me."

Griffin smiled and chugged down his beer. "Two shots of whiskey," he said to the bartender. "Let's make this interesting. See who's man enough to do the most shots."

"That's juvenile," Dave said. "I'm fine with just my beer."

The shots arrived pronto.

"Wimp." Griffin took a shot and slammed the shot glass on the bar. "Another." The bartender put another one in front of him. "Too bad you haven't got the balls to do a shot."

"Oh, I've got balls all right. Two huge ones." *Not really.* Dave grabbed the shot glass, tossed back the whiskey, and immediately started coughing as it burned its way down his throat. He bit back an exclamation and shook his head in a way he hoped passed for manly.

Griffin finished his second shot and eyed Dave. "If I hadn't gone on tour, you never would've been able to steal my woman."

Dave tapped his finger for another shot, already feeling more ballsy. The next shot arrived and Dave did that one with a minimal amount of coughing and pounding of chest. "You know what your problem is?" he asked Griffin in a loud voice.

Griffin raised a brow. "What's my problem, Dave?" he drawled.

"Too much touring, too little Steph." He grinned, the whiskey giving him more confidence. He was the guy for Steph, not Griffin. "I didn't steal her. She wasn't yours. You don't have a woman." He leaned closer to bring his point home. "At all."

"Oh, I've had women," Griffin growled. He turned to the bartender. "Four more, barkeep."

Dave's temper kicked up into the red zone. Griffin had all those women while he was still married to Steph. "I'll just bet you have. But not Steph. She's mine."

The shots arrived. Dave did another one and wiped his mouth. Shit. He felt light-headed. He grabbed some pretzels from the bowl sitting on the bar and shoved them in his mouth. The pretzels would absorb the alcohol. "And I've got something else you haven't got," he said over the pretzels in his mouth.

Griffin did another shot and gave him a sideways glance. "What's that, hotshot?"

Dave's tongue felt too big for his mouth. He finished another shot, wolfing down the pretzels. The words came slowly. "Numerical prowess. What's seven hundred thirty-one times fifty-seven?"

Griffin barked out a laugh. "You think Steph cares about that?"

Dave's words slurred, but he got them out. "Forty one thousand six hundred sixty-seven."

Griffin snorted. "Try woman prowess. That's what women like. They want a guy who knows what they're doing. Like I know all of Steph's hot spots. I'll bet you haven't even found the sweet spot yet, have you?"

The words hung in the air between them.

Griffin smirked. "I knew it!"

Dave launched himself at Griffin. They hit the ground, the

barstools flying across the room. They rolled all over the floor, a tangle of limbs. Dave had Griffin's long hair fisted in one hand, and he struggled to get his other arm out of Griffin's ironclad grip so he could get in one good punch to that pretty boy's face.

"Whoa, Griffin Huntley's in a bar fight," someone yelled. "Say cheese." A flash went off.

They rolled some more. More flashes went off. Some beeps too as cell phones recorded the epic event. *Ha!* Dave thought, somewhat deliriously. *This will be all over the tabloids. I'll definitely be called to the principal's office!*

Griffin loosened his grip on Dave to glare at the crowd hovering nearby. "No pictures!" Griffin hollered. "No video!"

Dave took advantage of the distraction and rolled off Griffin, intent on getting away from the man he never should've taken on, when his elbow accidentally hit Griffin in the face. Suddenly blood spurted out of Griffin's nose.

"You broke my nose!" Griffin screamed. He staggered to his feet. Someone handed him a napkin, and he tilted his head back, trying to stop the bleeding.

Dave stood, horrified. "I didn't..." He trailed off as the blood oozed through the white napkin, making him feel woozy. "Shit," he said before he passed out.

When he came to, Griffin was glaring at him, holding an ice pack to his nose, and a tough-looking police officer was staring down at him.

"Can you stand?" the cop asked.

Dave stood, veering unsteadily to the side. The cop's name tag said R. O'Hare. R. O'Hare was going to arrest him. Him, a respectable teacher, in jail. He felt a little woozy again. He focused away from the sharp eyes of the cop, willing himself to stay upright.

"You two are spending the night in a very special place where you can cool off," R. O'Hare said.

"I'm not going anywhere," Griffin said in a big show of tough-guy bravado that Dave felt was ill-advised, even in his barely coherent state.

R. O'Hare was unimpressed. "We've already got drunken

and disorderly conduct and disturbing the peace. You want to add some more charges to the list?" At Griffin's silence, R. O'Hare jerked his head to the door. "Didn't think so. Let's go."

Dave went peacefully.

"I want a lawyer," Griffin said, digging in his heels.

"You'll get your phone call," R. O'Hare said. "Now let's go," he bit out, "or do I need to cuff you?" He glanced meaningfully around at all the patrons eagerly watching the scene.

Griffin went. R. O'Hare ushered them into the back of his police car and made the short drive to the Clover Park police station.

"What do we have here, Chief?" another cop asked.

"Two drunk idiots. Put them in the holding cell to sober up."

Dave would've normally been mortified to be in jail, terrified to be locked up with his arch enemy, but he was much too busy trying not to puke.

7

Steph showed up at the Clover Park police station at six a.m. Saturday morning to talk to the two men that were a complete embarrassment to the male species and to her. Dave had called her last night making absolutely no sense. He just kept repeating, "I'm in jail, and I love your hair." Finally he must've handed the phone over because then Ryan O'Hare explained the situation. They'd agreed it was better to let the pair sober up overnight before letting them loose on Clover Park. Jaz had called right after. Her sister, Zoe, had been waitressing at Garner's and had seen the whole thing. Jaz told her all about how Dave had kicked Griff's ass. What did it say about Steph that she felt a little thrill that Dave had fought for her and won?

She should be furious with both of them for such a display. For getting shit-faced together. What were they doing together in the first place? This whole thing made her realize that the two men she'd thought were so different, actually had something more than just her in common. Griff had this alpha male thing going on with a hidden sweet side while Dave had a sweet personality with a hidden alpha. She'd thought she was getting the opposite of Griff with Dave, but now she wasn't so sure.

She pushed past a group of reporters that hovered by the

entrance of the town's police station and, finding the front door locked, rang the buzzer to be let in.

The deputy on duty, Matt, let her in, and the door locked shut behind her. "Those reporters showed up awful early," Matt said.

"Vultures," Steph said.

"They're in the holding cell in the basement." Matt gestured for her to follow. "Chief O'Hare's got no patience for drunks. These two passed out shortly after they got in."

She walked downstairs into a damp, dimly lit basement with one jail cell. Kinda creepy. She peered in the cell. Griff was sprawled on the cot, hands behind his head, looking for all the world like he was relaxing poolside. Dave was sitting on a wooden bench, head in his hands.

"I asked Chief O'Hare not to release you until I could talk to you," Steph said.

Matt stepped back, giving them some space.

"Steph." Dave leapt to his feet, then winced and held his head.

"Hey, babe," Griff said, sitting up and taking his time getting over to her. Omigod. His nose was swollen, and he had a black eye. Dave really did kick his ass. Her gaze trailed back to Dave, who slowly made his way over. Look at that badass. She licked her lips as she took in Dave's rumpled hair, his stubble, his broad shoulders, the trim physique that was full of power. A thrill ran through her. *Cool it. This is wrong.* What Griff and Dave did was *wrong.* So why was she so turned on?

Steph gave them each a hard look. "The entire town is talking about your barroom brawl. It's completely embarrassing. I teach their children! No more fighting. You're two grown men in your thirties, who are way too old to be getting drunk and taking shots at each other. You especially, Griff. This is all over the Internet."

Griff rubbed his stubbled jaw. "What are they saying?"

"They're saying you got your ass kicked by a middle school math teacher."

Dave's chest puffed out.

"It was a lucky shot," Griff said. "Let me out of here, Steph. I've got some serious damage control to do with my people."

"Not until you promise me"—she pointed her finger at both of them—"no more fighting."

Dave held up a hand. "I swear. No more fighting. I don't know what came over me."

"Thank you," Steph said. She turned to Griff.

"Whatever," Griff grumbled.

"No, not 'whatever,'" Steph said, completely out of patience. "Promise! And promise you'll sign those divorce papers too!"

Griff scowled.

"I swear I'll leave you in here to rot!" Steph hollered. "I want your word, Griffin Huntley!"

Griff cringed over her yelling. "All right, all right, I promise."

"To both things," she clarified. "No fighting and sign the papers."

"Yeah, yeah," Griff muttered.

"Good." She turned and called to the deputy, "Matt, you can let them out now."

"Got it." Matt, seemingly used to holding drunks from Garner's for the night, casually walked over and unlocked the cell. "Don't let me see your faces in here again."

"No, sir," Dave said.

Griff gave a mock salute and sauntered out. Once they'd gotten their possessions back, Griff stayed behind to call his driver, and probably his manager, lawyer, and publicist too. She figured he wouldn't face the reporters waiting outside without a game plan.

Dave held Steph's hand. His larger hand enveloped hers in warmth. "Sorry."

She shook her head. "Things like this always seem to happen when Griff's around."

"You'll never have to bail me out of jail again. Promise."

"I know."

They walked outside into a crisp October day.

Dave squinted at the morning light. "I never should've done shots."

She ran her hand up and down his arm. "You think you'll be up to getting together later?"

He swallowed. "Uh, yeah. Tonight?"

"Maybe sooner. Afternoon?" She ran her fingers through his hair.

He gazed down at her. "Sooner's good."

"My place. I'll be waiting for you…naked."

"I'll be there," he said in a strained voice.

"Good," she purred.

"Now that's what I'm talking about," Griff said when Steph answered the door naked later that day.

She gawked. Griff had cut his long hair in a short, close-cropped style, and he was clean-shaven. She'd never seen him like that. He looked younger, sweeter. Except for the black eye.

"I feel overdressed," he said with a grin.

She slammed the door, face flaming. She grabbed the blanket from the sofa and wrapped it around her. Someone must've let him up because the buzzer hadn't rung. She should tell her neighbors only to let Dave up, but everyone in town was fascinated with Griff. Her neighbors kept asking about him, her coworkers, even the principal. Jaz told her people at Garner's were betting—Team Dave vs. Team Griffin. She was mortified by all the talk. She'd moved here to get away from all that. Anyway, she was one hundred percent Team Dave.

And what were the odds of Griff showing up at her apartment on a Saturday afternoon? She'd thought he'd be gone by now. And why had he suddenly shed his famous locks? All that hair. That beautiful hair.

"Babe," he called through the door. "Don't be shy. You're looking good. Just like I remember."

He was being kind. Her body wasn't what it was five

years ago, but she smiled a little, appreciating the sentiment. She really had to get him out of here before Dave arrived.

She opened the door again. "You look so different. Why the change?"

"Can I come in?" he asked. "Seems like you were hoping I'd show up."

She let out a breath of exasperation and let him in. "Obviously I wasn't expecting you."

He gave her a quick up and down, lingering on her cleavage. She wrapped the blanket a little higher around her.

She met his eyes, and he gave her a slow, sexy smile. She still couldn't get over this new look. He looked like a clean-cut guy, not the badass rocker she knew him to be. She'd be lying if she said his new look was unappealing. The swelling on his nose had gone down too.

He ran his fingers through his short hair. "I feel like I shed twenty pounds." He laughed.

She stared.

He crossed to her, stepping into her personal space. "I wanted to show you I can change."

She swallowed hard. She didn't know what to say. A haircut didn't mean he was a different person. But he just looked so different. He looked like the sweet boy she'd seen in some of his mother's photo albums. Little Griffin smiling at the keyboard.

He pushed a lock of her hair back and it brushed over her bare shoulder, reminding her she was nearly naked with the wrong man.

"What are you doing here?" she asked. "I thought you were flying back this afternoon."

"The gig fell through," he said. "I've got another week. I want to spend some time with you. Just the two of us."

"No."

"Steph," he said softly. "Come on." She was overwhelmed with his scent of leather and freshly showered male. "What are you afraid will happen if you're alone with me?"

She said nothing.

"What do you hope will happen?" he asked in a sultry voice.

She met his eyes and said in a cool voice, "I'm over you, Griff. Nothing will happen."

He gave her a pleading expression, looked deep into her eyes, and said the one word she never, ever heard from him, "Please."

Still, she needed to move on, not get tangled up with him further.

She shook her head. "I'm done. It took me a long time to get over you." She gave him a hard look. "A long, painful time. But I did. And I'm not going back. I'm with Dave now. Nothing you say or do will change that. Please let me move on with my life."

He cradled her cheek with one hand. At his touch, she remembered vividly his gentle, sweet side. The many times he'd cradled her cheek, always before—

"I still love you," he said, gazing into her eyes.

Before he said something from the heart.

She backed away, tripping on the area rug, and would've toppled over, but he reached out and righted her. She straightened the blanket and stood stiffly. "It's too late for that." She took another step back, because memories of a long ago time didn't make up for the years between. "I love Dave."

A flash of hurt crossed his face before he dropped his gaze, staring at the floor. He heaved a sigh and rubbed the back of his neck. He looked at her. She looked steadily back.

"We're going to visit your brother tomorrow," he said. "You and me. His family."

Her stomach twisted. "Joey's not your family. Not anymore."

"Last time I visited, he told everyone I was his big brother."

Her jaw dropped. "You visited him? When?"

"Last year when I was on the East Coast."

Griff was an only child. It must have meant a lot to him to have a little brother, even if it was only by marriage. She suddenly found herself choked up.

"I didn't know you visited," she said over the lump in her throat. "How long have you been doing that?"

"I never stopped."

Steph blinked, suddenly hurt. Griff had visited her brother for years, and not her? Joey only lived two hours away from her.

"If I'd known, I would've met up with you guys," she said softly.

Griff shoved his hands in his pockets. "I knew I didn't deserve you. I'm sorry, Steph. For everything."

She studied him for a moment. "Okay."

He met her eyes with a pained expression. "I never really gave our marriage a chance. I regret that. Very much. It was all my fault."

She softened at his words. "It was all your fault."

"So will you come with me tomorrow? Joey always asks about you when I visit. What does he know about how complicated relationships are? As far as he knows, we're married, so that makes us all family."

She nodded. "Yeah, I'll go."

"Go where?" a voice asked from behind Griff.

"Dave!" Steph exclaimed. "I didn't hear the buzzer." One of her neighbors must've been Team Dave and let him up.

Dave took in her blanket, still showing lots of leg because she had to cover her cleavage and the blanket only stretched so far, took in Griff, and narrowed his eyes. "Your neighbor let me in. What's going on here?"

"Griff was just leaving," she said.

Griff inclined his head. "See you tomorrow, sweetheart." He smiled smugly at Dave, who scowled back.

Steph followed Griff to the door, locked it behind him, and turned to face Dave. His jaw was clenched tight as he took in her nearly naked state. She wasn't sure if he was going to yell at her or tear the blanket off and have his way with her. She knew which one she wanted.

She dropped the blanket.

∾

Dave closed his eyes, torn between his baser urges and the need to find out what the hell Steph was doing with Griff just now and what she was planning to do with Griff tomorrow. He rubbed his temples hard. Think. All the blood had drained from his brain. But he was still seeing red. Their first time shouldn't be angry sex. Right?

Her arms wrapped around his waist as she pressed herself against him. Instinct took over. He grabbed the back of her head and kissed her hard, long, and deep, nearly out of his mind to have her. To claim her. He shoved the coffee table out of the way. Within seconds, he had her on the floor, his pants halfway down. He felt like an animal, but he couldn't stop, and he couldn't slow down. He thrust his hand between her legs, felt the wetness there, heard her moan dimly in the roar of blood rushing in his ears just before he settled between her thighs and drove deep.

The feel of her so hot, so tight around him broke the last of his control. He slammed into her, taking what was his, vaguely aware of her legs wrapping around him, her nails digging into his shoulders. Their bodies, slick with sweat, slammed together again and again, until he thrust deep one final time as he exploded inside her with a roar. He collapsed on top of her, spent.

She was pushing at his shoulders, and he belatedly realized he was crushing her. He propped his weight up on his elbows and looked down at her. Her lips were rosy, swollen from his kisses. He wanted to apologize for the way he took her, so fast, too rough, but what came out was the truth.

"You're mine," he said. He was still buried deep inside her.

She stared at him in wonder. "I didn't know you had it in you. That was so…intense."

He gazed into her eyes. "You're mine. Not Griffin's. I need to hear you say it."

"I'm yours," she said.

He relaxed again, kissed her tenderly, and wished he could just let it go at that. Even knowing it would make him mad all over again, he had to know. "Tell me what you're doing with Griffin tomorrow."

She stroked his hair. "We're visiting my brother."

"I thought Griffin was leaving."

"He's here another week."

He grunted, not happy with that. "I'll go with you."

She kissed him, her hot tongue stroking him, and he felt himself pulse inside her, growing harder again. "I don't want fighting in front of my brother," she whispered near his ear. "It'll be okay."

He was about to roll off her, irritated with himself for wanting her when she was clearly playing with him, when she informed him, "I'm on the pill and healthy, just so you know. So we can—"

"Fuck," he muttered. "Birth control." He couldn't believe he'd forgotten that. He never forgot.

She laughed. "Yes, fuck."

He let out a breath. "I'm healthy too."

"Good." She cupped his ass and squeezed.

He bit back a groan. This was not good. The wanting. The sharing her with another man.

"Maybe you should work things out with your husband," he said, hating himself for saying that when he loved her so damn much.

"Don't you give up on me!" she exclaimed just as she smacked his ass with both hands, hard enough to sting. Instinctively, he thrust inside her, hard and deep. She moaned and looked at him, challenge in her hazel eyes. "Teach me, Dave. Teach me that I'm yours."

Raw desire pounded through him. He stood, kicked off his jeans and boxers, and pulled her to her feet. Dave was not one to back down from a challenge. Or a teachable moment.

～

Steph lay down on the bed and watched as Dave set his glasses on the nightstand and pulled his T-shirt over his head.

"Steph," he said in a low, husky voice. "I'm honored that you chose me."

Tears unexpectedly stung her eyes. *Honored.* He made it sound like she was something precious. He settled on the bed next to her, lying on his side. She reached for him, and they connected with a white-hot heat as their lips found each other. His large, warm hands roamed over her body as they kissed, and she lost herself in his taste, his touch, this fire burning between them.

"You're mine," he murmured before brushing his lips across hers. "All mine." Then his mouth claimed hers, hard and demanding again, and she surrendered with a sigh. His hands slowed, stroking her back, as his mouth slanted over hers again and again. She pulled at him, wanting him on top of her, inside her, and he complied, settling between her legs. But then he nuzzled into her neck, kissing and licking, before working his way down her body, from her collarbone down to her breasts, where he lingered, drawing her nipple into his mouth, making her hips move side to side restlessly.

"Dave," she gasped as his teeth scraped against her sensitive nipple. "I want you inside me."

He tsked. "I'm teaching you. That's what you wanted." He suckled the other breast, using his teeth and tongue, and the throbbing between her legs intensified. She was going to come if he didn't stop. She wanted him, needed him, inside her.

"Forget the teaching," she gasped out.

He moved back to kiss her, sucking her lower lip into his mouth. He released her and gazed down at her lips. "Mine. My mouth. Say it's mine. No one else kisses you."

"Yours," she said on a sigh. She never should've asked him to teach her she was his. Now he would be slow and thorough like his kissing usually was. She was so turned on already.

He ran his tongue along her earlobe. "Mine," he growled.

"Yours," she said. She moved her hips restlessly against him, desperate for more. His palm flattened against her hip, holding her still.

He kissed along her neck, his teeth scraping her with a delicious thrill. "Mine."

She sighed.

His teeth held her by the side of the neck, waiting.

"Yours," she finally gasped out. She tangled her hands in his hair. "Please," she begged, but he wasn't done teaching her.

His hand cupped her breast. He dipped his head, flicking his tongue over her erect nipple. "Mine."

"Yours," she said immediately.

He rewarded her quick response with deep suction that had her crying out. Her nails dug into his back as the pressure built on the edge of release, but then he stopped. She panted as he moved to the other breast, cupping it. He looked into her eyes, waiting.

"Yours," she quickly said.

"Good," he murmured, before he gave that breast the same treatment, sucking and grazing her with his teeth, making her arch up into him. Her insides clenched, the pressure built unbearably, and then when she was teetering right there on the peak of what promised to be a hell of a climax, he stopped. Her eyes flew open, and she caught his small smile. He knew she was on the edge; he was deliberately holding her back. He kissed his way down her stomach and his tongue dipped into her navel. Before she could yell at him to stop teasing her, he shifted lower and pressed a kiss to her center.

"Yours, yours, yours," she cried.

His fingers dipped lower, sliding up and down her slick folds. "Who touches you here?"

"You."

"Only me. This is mine."

"Yes."

His fingers slipped inside her, stroking her on the inside. She bucked her hips. He pressed in further, his thumb resting on her hard nub, and held her firmly. "All of this is mine."

She panted, tossing her head side to side because the rest of her was caught in his large hand. Close, she was so close.

"Look at me," he said. "Your orgasms are mine. *Every one.*"

She opened her eyes at his intense gaze and whimpered. His thumb applied pressure, and she gasped. She bucked her hips, needing more. "Yours," she said, but it was more a command than a submission. She wanted what the word gave her.

His hand released her, and she nearly cried from the loss, but then he shifted, moving down her body, and his mouth closed over her center. She cried out, and he stopped.

"Please, don't stop," she gasped out.

"Mine," he said, blowing over the sensitive nub.

She trembled. "Yours."

He lapped at her, making her writhe underneath him. Then he suckled, and she arched against his mouth. Her nails dug into his shoulders as the pressure built, spiraling quickly out of control.

He lifted his head, using his fingers to stroke her in slow, lazy circles. His voice sounded distant as she was consumed, all of her senses focused on his fingers. "Say my name when you come," he commanded.

She whimpered.

"Mine," he growled before he took her fully in his mouth, his tongue hard against her most sensitive spot.

"Dave," she cried out as she broke in a rush, thrashing wildly as she rode every last wave against his demanding mouth.

She lay there, panting, when he finally released her. She felt his heat, his weight, as he settled over her.

"Very good." His voice rumbled near her ear. "You get an A plus."

She smiled and then gasped as he drove deep. She arched her hips, wrapping her legs around him, and he sank deeper. They both groaned.

"You're mine," she said.

His forehead rested against hers, and he kissed her tenderly. "Yours."

He moved in a slow and steady rhythm that had her eyes

rolling back in her head. The pressure built again, and she felt herself hurtling toward another climax as he thrust harder and faster.

"Open your eyes," he said.

Her eyes fluttered open to find his blue eyes, dark with desire, gazing down at her fiercely. The effect was intense, the intimacy of that moment. She cried out his name as she went over the edge, and he followed after with a groan.

A few moments later, he propped up his weight on his arms and kissed her gently. "Are you really going without me tomorrow?"

"Dave," she said quietly. She didn't want to fight. Not now. She just wanted to enjoy this moment.

He smiled mischievously before he leaned down to suck on her neck. Hard.

"Dave!"

He released her and looked down at her neck. He grinned. "Looks like you're mine."

She smacked his arm. "I can't believe you gave me a hickey!"

He stared at it with satisfaction. "Looks like you've been thoroughly worked over. Where else can I mark you?"

"Don't you dare!"

He rolled off her, chuckling. Then he pulled her close so her head was resting on his chest and pulled the covers over them. She sighed, feeling relaxed and satisfied.

His hand cupped her ass. "You shouldn't dare me, you know. That feels like a challenge I can't back down from." He gave her ass a squeeze. "I could mark you here."

Her voice came out shaky. "Don't you dare."

"I told you not to dare me," he said in a voice laced with dark intent.

She felt the moment he was going to move out from under her, but before he could, she looped her arms around his neck and sucked his neck hard. She pulled back and looked at him with satisfaction. "Now we're even."

"Ouch," he said, holding his hand against the side of his

neck. It was a good one too. Nice and big. "You sucked a lot harder than I did."

She laughed.

He shook his head, a small smile playing over his lips. "I love you, Steph."

She beamed. "I love you too."

He propped up on one elbow, facing her, and pushed a lock of hair over her ear. "I want a future with you."

"Aww, I want that too."

He rubbed her hair between his fingers. "You know before I found out you were married, I'd planned on proposing. I was even researching diamond rings."

"Oh, Dave," she said over the lump in her throat. "I would've said yes if I could have."

He frowned and looked down before finally saying, "This whole thing with Griffin is really hard for me. I hate it. I really do."

She stroked his arm. "I know. I wish I'd met you five years ago instead."

He met her eyes. "If you do marry me some day, I will never, ever leave you. I will *always* be faithful. You can count on that. I'll spend every day making sure you know just how special you are to me."

She blinked back tears. "See? If I met you five years ago, it would've saved me years of heartbreak. My life would've been so much better with you."

He cursed under his breath. Then he pulled her on top of him and smiled wickedly. "I'm gonna make sure you're walking funny when you see Griffin tomorrow."

"I dare you," she returned.

Famous last words.

8

Steph heard the buzzer the next morning and hit the button to let Griff up. Dave stopped her halfway to the front door with a hand on her arm. "I'll get it, honey."

She shot him a look. "No fighting."

"You should wear your hair up." He lifted her hair and ran a finger down the side of her neck where he'd marked her.

"No need. Yours is like a flashing neon sign."

He self-consciously put a hand to his neck. She laughed. He grabbed her, nipping her bottom lip and sucking it into his mouth. She merely pressed herself against him. He had a possessive, jealous streak that brought out the animal in him. She loved it.

Griff knocked. Dave didn't release her. Instead he slanted his mouth over hers in a hard kiss that had her moaning in his mouth.

Griff knocked again. Dave's hand slid down her ass and rocked her into him. His tongue was doing a perfect imitation of the hard thrusting he'd treated her to multiple times last night and this morning.

"Steph?" Griff called.

She tore her mouth from Dave's and went to answer the

door. Dave picked her up by the waist and set her down behind him. He pulled open the door. "Hey, Griffin."

Griff took in Dave's wet hair, fresh from the shower, his wrinkled T-shirt, jeans, and bare feet. "Ready to go, Steph?" he asked, leaning to look past Dave to Steph.

"Sure, let me just grab my purse." She stopped in the kitchen where she'd dropped it on the counter and heard Dave in full peacock mode.

"She might be walking a little funny after last night. Right, babe?"

She restrained herself from the eye roll she longed to do. Jealous and possessive was fun in bed, especially the multiple ways Dave wanted to claim her and remind her she was his, but in front of Griff, it was a little embarrassing. She returned to the two men to find Griff, nostrils flaring, in a staring contest with Dave.

"All ready," she said, holding up her purse.

"Call me when you get home," Dave said. "We'll have dinner." Then he bent her over his arm to kiss her long and deep. She heard Griff mutter a curse, but Dave wasn't done reminding her she was his. Finally, he let her back up, his eyes burning into hers.

Griff had stepped out into the hallway, his back to them.

She smoothed her hair, a little breathless. "I'll call you."

He grunted his approval. She turned, and he smacked her ass on the way out. She yelped.

"Mine," he growled.

Her cheeks flushed over the testosterone-fueled posturing, even as she felt herself go damp.

"Yours," she muttered over her shoulder before heading out the door with her husband.

The silence stretched awkwardly between Steph and Griff on the limo ride to Horizon Village. She knew Dave hadn't helped matters, but at least he and Griff hadn't gotten physical. Steph sat on the far edge of the long wraparound bench seat from Griff. He stretched out his long legs, leaned his head back, and put his aviator shades on. She studied him for a few minutes as his breathing deepened. He was still clean-shaven. He reminded her a little of Dave now with his squeaky clean good looks.

Griff appeared to be sleeping. She was tired too. Dave woke her up twice last night with a rumbled "mine" in her ear as his hands and mouth staked his claim. Not that she minded, but she was tired, and it was a two-hour drive. She curled up on her side on the long bench seat and fell asleep.

She woke to the feel of someone stroking her hair, and she snuggled into the warm lap her head was now resting on. Her mother always used to stroke her hair to wake her. Slowly she opened her eyes to find Griff gazing down at her.

"Hey, sleepyhead," he said.

She scrambled to sit upright. "What happened? How long was I sleeping? Where are we?"

"Chill. You slept for an hour and a half. We're almost there."

She shifted a little further away from him and smoothed her hair. "How did I get my head in your lap?"

He chuckled. "I just let you rest your head on my leg as a pillow. You're the one that shifted into more interesting parts."

"Griff!" she snapped, but that was as far as she got before he kissed her. It was a tender kiss that her body remembered even as her mind rebelled. She pushed on his chest, and he leaned back on the seat. "Don't."

"Did you feel something?" he asked.

She shook her head quickly to deny it. "No."

"I did." He studied her a moment. "You're lying. I know you, Steph. We've always had chemistry."

"I've got that plus more with Dave," she said. Dave offered stability, faithfulness, and, one day she hoped, a family they'd raise together. He'd make a wonderful father. Griff could never match that.

He took her hand and held it warmly between his. She tried to pull it back, but he wasn't letting go.

"When we first met," he said, "I had nothing. Just a tiny apartment I shared with Henry and Jake."

She remembered. That closeness between him and his bandmates probably contributed to their great work together musically.

He squeezed her hand and spoke in earnest. "I can give you so much more now. Whatever you want. I have a beach house in Laguna Beach, a house in Aspen, we could get one in Clover Park. You could join me on tour in the summer when you're off from work. We could have kids like you always wanted."

Her heart ached hearing those words from him now. Kids. One of the things they'd fought about just before his band hit big. Her wanting them, him not wanting them.

"And the kids would see you when?" she asked. More of a rhetorical question than anything else. She wouldn't be having Griff's children.

He held out his palms, releasing his hold on her hand. "Whenever they liked. We could get a nanny and a tutor, total freedom. You wouldn't have to work another day in your life."

An offer some women would jump at. Just not her. "That's not what I want. I love teaching. I want to raise my kids in a small town like Clover Park with a dad that's there for them day in and day out for tying shoelaces and packing lunches and bedtime stories—everything. Someone to teach them and love them."

His mouth curled in disgust. "Like Dave? What's he gonna teach them, how to get beat up in gym class?"

A cold fury ran through her. "We're done, Griff. It's time you accepted that."

Griff's lips formed a flat line. Steph turned away.

"Joey's tuition is expensive," Griff said.

She turned back. "What are you trying to say?"

He turned and stared out the window. Steph worried her lower lip. Was Griff trying to say that he'd stop paying the tuition if she divorced him? She had to find a way to keep things steady for Joey no matter what happened. Her brother did not deal well with changes in his routine. He'd thrown tantrums for a month when they'd first moved him to Horizon Village. He'd almost been kicked out. And a grown man, even a short one, could be strong and destructive when throwing a tantrum. She'd need someone to watch him during the day if he had to move in with her. Or she'd have to take a lot of time off work. Her stomach twisted. She couldn't afford any of those options.

Griff stared out the window of the limo. He was at a crossroads. Mandy was driving the limo so she could get pictures of him and Steph with Joey. Steph's weakness was her brother. Would offering to pay his tuition win him Steph, or would threatening not to pay the tuition keep her married to him? A grateful Steph would be easier to live with. As they got closer to Horizon Village, he could tell she was worried. He'd let her stew so she'd be even more grateful in the end. He'd always pay Joey's tuition as long as he could afford it. He loved Joey like a brother. That didn't mean he would make it easy for Steph to walk away from him.

He knew she'd fucked Dave. He didn't like it, but he was willing to forgive it in light of his string of women. He'd go cold turkey on the women if he could just get Steph back. He'd never been more inspired musically than when he was with her.

Steph knocked on the door of her brother's group home. She'd called ahead so he'd be expecting her. She could hear some excited voices, and then the door swung open.

Joey beamed a smile at her. "Stephanie!"

"Hi, Joey," she said, reaching down to hug her much shorter brother. "I missed you."

He stood back and smiled, ear to ear. He looked at Griff and held up his hand for a high five. "Big brother!"

"Joey, my man," Griff said with an enthusiastic high five.

Steph's heart squeezed as Griff and Joey smiled at each other. Her brother's dark brown hair was combed neatly to the side. His eyes were hazel like hers, but rounder, and he wore thick glasses. Some of Joey's housemates came to the door.

"Who's this?" one young man asked.

"Stephanie and Griff," Joey said proudly. "My family."

Griff's hand settled on her shoulder and squeezed. Steph smiled tightly. After they'd met and been introduced to Joey's three housemates (who Steph had met before on several occasions, but Joey wanted to introduce them again), they went for a walk on the grounds. It reminded Steph a little of a college campus with manicured lawns and lots of trees.

"How's rock and roll?" Joey asked.

"It's awesome, buddy," Griff replied. "I even wrote a new song a few days ago, inspired by your sister."

Steph jolted. He was still writing songs for her?

"Play it," Joey said.

Griff shook his head. "I didn't bring my guitar, but you know what?"

"What?" Joey asked with a big smile.

"You'll hear it on the radio soon."

"Awesome!" Joey exclaimed, raising his hand for another high five. Griff gave him five. "With Twisted Star?"

"Yes, with Twisted Star. Hey, how's that keyboard I got you?"

"Awesome!" Joey exclaimed, high-fiving Griff.

Steph listened as Joey and Griff talked, slowly realizing that Griff had not only sent gifts, but also visited frequently and called. Maybe that was Griff's intention, to let her know how much he'd done for her brother. Even so, she couldn't help but love him for it. Not everyone understood how special Joey was. Griff seemed to genuinely care about him.

She cocked her head to the side, catching a glimpse of someone in a hoodie standing across the lawn, half hidden by a tree. She swore it was the same hoodie person she'd seen at her house and outside of Garner's that night when both Dave and Griff had performed. She grabbed Joey's hand.

"Show me that keyboard, Joey," she urged, pulling him back toward the house. "I can't wait to hear you play it."

"I play with drums sound," he said.

"You do? That's awesome." She hurried him along, her eye on the person in the hoodie, who seemed to be following them. "What songs do you know?"

"Yes," Joey said. Sometimes if Joey didn't know how to answer a question, he just said yes.

"What's wrong?" Griff asked.

Steph jerked her head toward the person following them.

Griff shook his head. "I don't know how they find me."

"What's wrong?" Joey echoed. He stopped and looked up at Steph with wide eyes. "Everything okay?"

"Yes, everything's okay," Steph said, pulling him along again. She wasn't so sure it was a coincidence that the hoodie person had found Griff here. Maybe Griff wanted pictures of the three of them together for some reason.

They went back to the house, where Griff and Joey played on the keyboard together, singing some of Twisted Star's songs. Joey knew a lot of the words, which meant he must've listened to them a lot. She hadn't realized what an important part of Joey's life Griff was. She should introduce Joey to Dave soon. Dave was her future.

After their visit, which Steph enjoyed more than she'd ever thought she could with Griff along for the ride, she slipped back into the limo with Griff.

"That was fun," Griff said as the limo pulled away. He stretched his arms out along the bench seat, his fingers brushing her hair. He rubbed a lock between his thumb and forefinger. "Like old times, huh, Steph?"

"I appreciate how good you are to him," she said. "He's—"

"Special," Griff finished for her.

Tears stung her eyes. "He is."

"I know. I love him too."

Her heart squeezed. She nodded, unable to speak over the lump in her throat.

"Steph, about Joey…"

Her heart sped up. "What about him?"

"As long as I can afford it, divorce or not, I'll pay his tuition. I'll try to keep the celebrity charity events going too. That's the easiest way for me to get the cash to Horizon Village."

Relief rushed through her. "Oh, Griff, you know how much this means to me. And to him." She took a shaky breath and for the first time in a long time looked at him with something other than anger or aggravation. "Thank you."

He settled his hand on her shoulder and squeezed. "You're welcome." He let go of her shoulder and leaned toward the minibar. "You want a drink?"

"No, thanks."

He poured himself a shot of whiskey and tossed it back. "Sometimes I think I would've been happier if I was still a guitar teacher, you know? Building a life with you."

A loud click sounded. Did the doors just lock? She slowly leaned toward the handle and tested it. Locked. Her eyes flew to his.

"Don't worry about it," he said. "The driver locked it for safety. You don't want to fly out on the freeway, do you?"

She settled uneasily back in the seat.

"We're having dinner at Grinaldi's," he informed her. "Skyline view."

"I promised to meet Dave for dinner," she said.

He raised a brow. "Call and tell him you can't make it."

"No."

He lifted one shoulder up and down.

She pulled her cell from her purse, hit Dave's number, when Griff snatched it out of her hand, tucking it into his back pocket. "Give that back!"

"You'll get it back after dinner."

"You can't kidnap me!"

Griff snorted. "It's just dinner."

"What do you want from me?"

"I want a second chance."

"You won't get one this way. You can't force someone to dinner and force them back into a marriage. It doesn't work that way!"

Steph fumed. She couldn't believe Griff was acting like this. Especially after he'd been so sweet to her brother. After he promised to take care of him no matter what. Was that his plan? To win her over through Joey? She wouldn't let him manipulate her that way.

"Griff, you don't have to take care of Joey after the divorce. I absolve you of all responsibility. Dave and I will take care of him."

Griff stared at her, incredulous. "You're turning down my money?"

Steph felt a little sick at the thought of uprooting Joey, but what could she do? This was wrong. Plain and simple.

"Yes," she said.

Griff was silent, looking out the window. He turned back to her. "You'd just let Dave take my place?"

"You can still have a relationship with Joey. He loves you. I won't stand between you. But, I won't let you use him to get to me."

The window separating them from the driver rolled down. "We have to stop for gas," a feminine voice said. "There's a lot of traffic up ahead. I don't want to stall out."

"Fine," Griff said.

"And then I need to go home," Steph said.

"We're skipping Grinaldi's," Griff added with a frown.

They pulled off at the next rest stop. The driver, a woman dressed plainly in a hoodie and jeans, opened the back door. "This thing takes a while to fill up. Why don't you get yourself a snack or something?"

Griff pulled Steph out of the car with him. "Come on."

She followed him to the small gas station mart. "Who is that? Why was she hiding behind a tree at Horizon Village?"

"Mandy. She's just part of the Griffin Huntley machine. She's harmless."

She glanced over her shoulder to find the woman

watching them. Griff slung his arm around her shoulder and whispered in her ear, "How about a Yoo-hoo?"

She laughed. He used to tease her about still liking Yoo-hoo chocolate drink as an adult. "I'd love one," she said.

He smiled down at her for a moment, then headed to the gas mart to get one. She was glad he seemed to have no hard feelings over her rejection.

❧

Dave was somewhere between jealousy and a white-hot rage after his sister emailed him the news story about Griffin and Stephanie. It was one of those stupid gossip websites talking about the famous couple getting back together. A rumor he could handle. That could be a lie. But this picture of Griffin and Steph didn't lie. Griffin had his arm around Steph, who was beaming up at him. Griffin was smiling down at her like she was his.

He took a few deep breaths, forcing himself to think rationally. There was only one explanation that made sense. Steph had lied to him. She'd said they were just visiting her brother. Yet she still wasn't back from what should've been a day trip. She was just hanging out with Griffin at sunset, smiling at him, letting him touch her.

Dammit. He should've known. How could he ever have thought for even one nanosecond that he could compete with Griffin Huntley, rock star? He was just a middle school math teacher. The most exciting thing he could offer Steph was help grading her papers.

His cell rang. Steph's number. He couldn't answer. He was too furious. He felt like a complete fool, and he wouldn't be able to stop himself from spewing his anger all over her. He quickly shut off the phone.

❧

Steph grew increasingly worried on the ride back home. Dave wasn't answering his cell. That wasn't like him. He was expecting her call, too.

"No answer, huh?" Griff asked. "He probably forgot to charge it."

"No, he charges it every night." She tried again and it went straight to voicemail. He wasn't answering the phone at his house either.

Griff started humming a melody to himself. "I wrote this song a few days ago. For you. It's called 'Missing Limb.'"

She wanted to cover her ears, as juvenile as that was. Then he sang about love and loss. About how he wished he had amnesia so he could forget her. About how she was a part of him. The best part.

What was she supposed to do about Griff? When he was focused on her, she felt the sincerity of his words, the love behind them. But once his attention shifted, it was like she didn't exist. All she wanted was a divorce so she could move on. Here he was, not wanting to let her go. He loved her in his way. It just wasn't the way she needed to be loved. And, in that moment, she finally understood that her marriage hadn't been a huge mistake, it had been founded in love. It just couldn't sustain itself through abandonment, betrayal, and multiple infidelities, she thought wryly. What marriage could?

"Did you like it?" he asked when he finished.

She forced a smile. "I think you've got another hit on your hands."

He slapped his leg and grinned. "I'm telling you, you're my muse, babe. I haven't written a new song in a year, and now they're just coming to me faster than I can get them down. Every morning I wake up with a new one in my head."

"I think it's time you found a new muse," she said gently.

He glanced at her. "No, babe. It's you. You're my good luck charm."

"So you're just going to hang around Clover Park writing new songs?"

"I have to go back to L.A. on Saturday. I mean, really have to. We've got a sold-out concert. I can't disappoint the fans."

"No, you certainly can't."

"But then I'll come back."

"No, Griff, don't. I don't know how to explain it any more clearly to you. I love Dave."

He heaved a sigh and drummed his fingers on the seat. Finally, he said, "I hope we can still be friends."

Relief surged through her. He got the message. "Okay, friends."

"Good."

After Griff dropped her off at home, Steph drove straight to Dave's place. As soon as he answered the door, she threw herself in his arms. He was stiff and not exactly hugging her back.

She pulled back. "I tried calling you, but it went to voicemail."

His jaw clenched. "I know."

"What happened? How come you didn't call me back?"

"Because I saw your picture with Griffin"—his voice rose to a roar—"and you looked pretty damn comfortable! Smiling! Touching! What am I supposed to think? What am I to you?"

"What picture?"

He pulled out his cell and showed her.

"Oh. I didn't know someone took a picture." It was probably the limo driver. Griff had said she was part of the machine. Now that she thought about it, Griff had seemed to be posing when he just stood there smiling at her. She put her hand on Dave's tense arm. "It was nothing. He said something funny about Yoo-hoo."

"There's nothing funny about Yoo-hoo," Dave spit out. "It's a delicious drink."

She bit back a smile. "I think the limo driver was trying to get a picture of us. Griff's using me for publicity. You know, the secret wife. I saw the limo driver at Horizon Village, hiding behind a tree. I bet she got some pictures of us with Joey."

He crushed her to him and kissed her. "I don't like this crazy business. Not one part of it."

"Me either."

He kissed her again. "Stay here until Griffin leaves." He kissed her for a very long time, and Steph finally felt like all was right in her world again.

She blinked slowly. "I have to go home for Loki."

"We'll stay at your place, then." He kissed her quick. "Let me pack a bag."

And, just like that, Dave moved in with her.

9

Dave spent the week acting like a total beast. The first night he was fine. Sure, he made love to Steph in an overbearing, possessive-freak way, but if her satisfied smile afterward was any indication, she was okay with that. But the second night, he saw a black sedan with tinted windows sitting outside her place, which triggered every protective instinct he had. There was no way he was letting Steph become a victim, stalked by the press, rumors and gossip ruining her good name.

He approached the car, intent on exercising Steph's right to privacy to Mandy, the celebrity gossip reporter Steph had told him about, but it wasn't a woman. It was Griffin. That man brought out the worst in Dave.

"What are you doing here?" Dave demanded.

"Nothing, man. Get lost."

"I will not get lost! You get out of here. Steph doesn't want to see you."

"Calm the fuck down. I'm not bothering anybody. I'm just writing music." He held up a small recorder and notepad.

"You're bothering me. Go write music somewhere else."

"Fuck you."

"Fuck you! I'm calling the cops. We're getting a restraining order."

"It's a public street. I can sit here if I want."

Dave stalked off and called the cops. A short while later, a cop arrived, and Griffin took off. Frustratingly, when Dave had told Steph to file a restraining order with the cop, she'd refused.

They had words. Fighting words.

"Dave," she said in an overly calm voice like he was an irrational child, "he won't hurt me. He's probably just writing music."

"He's obsessed with you."

She shrugged. "He thinks I'm his muse. He'll find a new muse and move on."

He put his hands on his hips. "When?"

"Hopefully by Saturday when he leaves."

Dave's blood was pounding in his ears. He couldn't believe Steph was so casual about Griffin basically stalking her. Was he supposed to just let the man sit out there every night watching the house?

"Fuck this," he said. "You're moving in with me."

"I'm not going anywhere. I don't understand why you're so mad. He's not dangerous."

Then it hit him with a sudden clarity. "You want him around! You like being his muse!"

"I want him to move on."

"Then file a restraining order!" he barked.

"No."

He had to take a walk to calm down. Call it insecurity. Call it jealousy. Call it the fucking power of love, but from the moment Dave got back from that walk, he couldn't keep his hands off Steph. Not as long as Griffin was still in the state of Connecticut.

As soon as he got back to Steph's place after work, he had her in bed, where he reminded her exactly whose she was. He knew he was being overbearing and way too demanding, he simply couldn't help himself. She didn't push him away either, which only made him want more. He invaded her shower every morning, kept her in her Columbia sweatshirt with nothing else so he could easily take her again and again. He felt like a damn rutting beast.

He could not stop.

And that fucking car sat outside every night. Steph wouldn't let him call the cops, which made him crazed, made him even more of a beast, until the car finally left.

Griffin never dared to come inside.

Griffin was out of time. It was Friday night, and he had to go back to L.A. for that concert tomorrow. Thousands of fans were waiting for him. The band was waiting for him. He parked in front of Steph's house in his rental car. He'd gotten the press his manager wanted. Tons of tabloids and gossip websites had the picture of him and Steph smiling at each other outside the gas station, his arm around her shoulders. Mandy got the shot and headed back to L.A. Job done.

Someone had dug up pictures of him and Steph on their honeymoon in Hawaii too, and pictures and video from the first tour he'd done. Probably his publicist. The headlines "Griffin Huntley's Secret Marriage," "Secret Wife Revealed," and "How Many Secret Wives are There?" with several of his lovers were just the boost that he'd needed. But instead of feeling satisfied, he just felt tired.

He was getting old. He wanted to stop all the touring. He missed the music. He missed his muse, Steph.

He knew Dave had spent the week at Steph's place. It was his penance to know. He accepted that as fitting punishment for all the affairs he'd had. Now he and Steph were even. They could move on. He intended to bring Steph back with him tomorrow, one way or another. He wanted her to see him in concert, to see him at his best. The music would bring them together.

Besides, his lawyer had told him a divorce would financially ruin him.

He nearly jumped out of his skin when the passenger-side

door opened and a petite woman with shoulder-length brown hair slid into the car. She turned to him. Shit. Dave's sister—the insane woman that jumped him outside of that bar.

"You!" he exclaimed.

One corner of her mouth lifted. "Me!" she mocked. She set a six-pack of lite beer on the console. "I thought we'd have a car party, instead of a stalking. Sound good?"

She popped open a can of beer and took a sip.

"Get out of my car, crazy lady."

She sipped her beer and eyed him with startlingly blue eyes. "Nope. Hey, let's play a game."

He shifted closer to the door.

"It's called, what's my name? Crazy lady doesn't count. And, for bonus points, why are you stalking my brother? The right answer means I don't call the cops." She gave him a serene smile that scared the shit out of him.

He couldn't remember her name. He met so many people he couldn't keep them straight, but he remembered that face with its blue eyes, sharp cheekbones, and even sharper tongue. That snarling New Yawk City accent. "Where're you from? Queens?"

"Brooklyn. Now answer the question."

"I'm not stalking your brother."

"*Brrrap.*" She made an obnoxious wrong buzzer sound. "See, when you hang out in front of Steph and Dave's place every night, that's called stalking."

He scowled. "I'm just writing music."

"Oh, very nice. And it's Christina. That's the last time I tell you that, so write it down if you have to. You still have my card?"

He shrugged.

She let out a huge sigh and dug another one out of her purse. "There. Last time you get one of those too."

He looked at it. Christina Righetti Olsen, R.N. There was a big black X through Righetti and Olsen was written in by hand diagonally between the Righetti and the R.N. She probably killed her first husband. Then it said: Home Health Care When You Need It Most. Her number too.

"When do you need home health care the most?" he asked.

"Weekends and nights. It's a side gig. I'm usually an oncology nurse at the hospital."

His eyes widened at the thought of Christina as a nurse. He couldn't imagine a less nurturing person to take care of sick people. He wouldn't let her in the room if he was on his deathbed.

"So, let's hear what you've got so far," she said.

When he just stared at her, she narrowed her eyes. "You're not really making music here, are ya?" She pulled out her cell. "I'll call the cops. Dave says Steph won't let him, but no one stops me."

"Wait!"

She smiled sweetly.

He glared at her. "You always get in your brother's business?"

She raised her brows. "I get in everyone's business."

He pulled his guitar from the back seat, tuned it, and sang her the song about Steph, "Missing Limb." He always loved an audience, even if it was just one person. He finished and looked over at her.

"That blows," she said.

He jerked back in surprise. Everyone loved his music.

She waved dismissively. "What else you got?"

"Who the hell asked you anyway?" he roared. That was the first song he'd written in a year, and she shot it down just like that. He'd like to hear her compose an original melody and the lyrics to go with it.

She cocked her head. "Your career's in a slump. You know why?"

"Enlighten me," he said through clenched teeth.

"Because you're still five years ago. You're playing the same old hits. Or variations of them."

"We just put out a new album last year."

"*Meh.* Warmed-up leftovers."

So furious he was almost shaking with it, he put his guitar

back in its case. He wasn't going to play one more note as long as *she* was in the car.

He had to force himself to unclench his jaw. "What do you know about music, Christina Olsen, R.N.? What the hell does a nurse know about music?"

She set her beer down in the cup holder and leveled him with a serious look. "I've been following your career since day one. I know your music very well. I love it. But it's time you pushed yourself. Take some risks. Break out from the pack."

"Easy for you to say," he muttered.

"I've got your poster on my bedroom wall. Know why?"

Now he was on more familiar ground. He gave her his slow, sexy smile. "I've got an idea."

She shook her head. "Yeah, you're pretty, but it's your eyes. They've got soul. They say to me, there's something beautiful and deep waiting to come out. I want to hear the music from your soul."

He scoffed. "That song I played was from my soul."

"Your music and your wife are five years ago. Stop living in the past."

"Shut up!" he barked. "You don't know anything about me and Steph!"

"Wake up!" she snapped and slapped him across the face.

He put his hand on his cheek in shock. It stung too. He was still gaping when she grabbed her beer and left.

Crazy lady. No one treated him like that. Especially not women. Women loved him. Christina had a screw loose.

Steph stretched like a contented cat on Saturday morning, Dave's hand possessively spread wide across her stomach. What a week. She smiled to herself. Griff hadn't bothered her. Dave couldn't get enough of her. She loved this fierce side to him. Slowly, ever so slowly, she slid out from under his hand and rolled out of bed. She headed for the bathroom, intent on surprising him. She quickly washed up and got to work.

It took a while, and it wasn't easy. But she thought it would be worth it. The door whipped open just as she put on the finishing touch.

His eyes took in her naked state and went dark with desire behind his glasses. His hair was adorably messy, sticking out every which way. "What are you doing out of bed?" he growled.

He liked to keep her in bed as much as possible. Except when she wanted to eat or watch TV or needed to grade papers. Even then, he liked to keep her close. She wasn't complaining.

She sauntered past him, stopped, and threw over her shoulder. "What do you think?"

She waited, her back to him so he could take in the rear view, and heard his sharp intake of breath.

"Steph, what did you do?"

She looked over her shoulder at his shocked expression and smiled to herself.

"Tell me that's not real," he said even as he was reaching out to her. He ran a finger along one butt cheek, tracing the D. She had a tattoo across both cheeks that said, Dave's.

"It's not real. And it wasn't easy to do reverse in the mirror." She huffed. "I hope you appreciate it."

He went down on his knees and kissed the D. She looked over her shoulder as he kissed every letter reverently. Heat pooled through her at his touch.

"I'm yours, Dave. All yours."

He stood with a groan, his hand still cupping her ass. "I've been a beast to you, and you never complained. You don't have to keep telling me you're mine."

She spread her legs and tipped forward, opening herself to him. "I loved every minute, you fucking beast."

He muttered a curse, grabbed her hips, and thrust fully inside her. It was fierce, urgent, and hot as all hell. His hands cupped her breasts, tugging on her nipples, as he thrust hard and steady.

"Mine," he said fiercely. She didn't know which part of her he was talking about, but it didn't matter, she was all his.

"Yours," she gasped out.

His fingers stroked her center, and she felt the familiar tightening as the pressure built. She closed her eyes, lost in sensation. His finger flicked across her hard nub, and she cried out.

"Mine," he said, flicking quickly over her again as he thrust steadily. Her entire body quivered.

"Yours," she cried out as the intensity skyrocketed with each flick of his finger. Her legs gave out, but he had her, one arm clamped around her waist. His touch gentled, stroking her center again, but his thrusts didn't let up, and she flew, as her body exploded with a climax that rushed through her, radiating out from her center all the way to her toes. His hands clamped on her hips, and she took in his last shuddering thrusts until he groaned, holding her tightly, as he let go deep inside her.

A moment later, he turned her in his arms and showered her with kisses—her eyelids, her cheeks, her lips, her chin. "I love you."

"I love you too."

He shook his head. "I still can't believe you chose me over him."

"You're the better man."

He wrapped his arms around her and held her tight for a few moments. He pulled back to look in her eyes. "How come you didn't have kids, you and Griffin?"

She looked down. "He didn't want them." She met his kind eyes. "I did. I've always wanted kids."

He cradled her face with both hands. "I want you to have my babies."

She blinked back tears.

"Or not. You don't have to." He stroked her cheek. "Don't cry."

She couldn't help it. Tears leaked out of her eyes even as she smiled. "I want that too."

"You do?" His eyes welled up, and he crushed her to him. "As soon as we're married."

She laughed. "I didn't hear a question in there."

He pulled back and grinned. "No, you didn't. Then we'll spend the summer on a long honeymoon at my family's cabin up at Lake George."

She ran her finger along his stubbled jaw. "I love all of that, but—"

He cut her off with a kiss that left her knees weak. When he let her up for air, she said, "But I still need that divorce."

Dave groaned. "He promised to sign the papers."

Her lips formed a flat line. "Griffin makes a lot of promises he doesn't keep."

"We'll get a good lawyer."

"Lawyers are expensive."

"So we just wait for Griffin to get off his ass and sign the papers? Fuck that."

She rubbed his chest, trying to soothe him. "I'll talk to him. He can be reasonable. We ended things as friends."

"And I'm supposed to wait around while you try to talk sense into him?" He jammed a hand in his hair. "How long am I supposed to wait?"

"Is there a time limit? Does your love expire?"

His jaw clenched, and a muscle ticked in his cheek. "Dammit," he muttered.

He pulled her into the bathroom, turned on the shower, and glowered at her while the water heated. She didn't say one word. She knew what was coming next. He pulled her in and was absolutely beastly to her.

Steph answered the door in her robe while Dave was still shaving. "Hi, Griff. Leaving today?"

His gaze dropped to her chest, and she tightened the robe around her.

His eyes met hers. "Today's the day."

"Don't forget you promised to sign those divorce papers."

"You really love him, huh?"

She raised her chin. "Yes, I do."

He heaved a sigh. "All right."

"All right?"

"Yeah, what can I do? I tried." His shoulders slumped, and he lost all traces of his usual arrogant swagger. "You know I'll always love you. Nothing I can do if you don't feel the same way…"

"Thank you."

He frowned. "Listen, I called Paulie D. He said the paperwork is complicated because, hell, I dunno, he just said it was complicated. But he'll take care of everything as soon as I say the word. You want this done fast? Fly back with me, and I'll have Paulie D bring the papers. I'll sign right there backstage after the concert."

Relief flooded through Steph. Tonight. She could have a divorce as soon as tonight.

"Okay, I'll go," she said.

He flashed a quick smile. "You will? Great. I've got a private jet. You'll love it."

"Sounds good. You know Dave will be with me."

He scowled. "You want to bring Dave."

"Yes." Two arms wrapped around her from behind. She could feel the heat of Dave's bare chest on her back. Dave rested his chin on her shoulder.

"Where we going, Griff?" Dave asked.

"Griff invited us to his concert tonight," Steph said brightly. "Then he promised to sign the divorce papers. We're flying on his private jet. Won't that be fun?"

Dave shifted to her side and draped an arm over her shoulders. He wore only jeans. "And do we believe that he will actually sign the papers?" He spoke to Steph, but never stopped glaring at Griff.

"I said I would, didn't I?" Griff snapped.

Steph turned to Dave. "It'll be fine." She turned to Griff. "We'll go."

"Can't wait," Dave said, only it came out sounding like *fuck you.*

"Let's go," Griff said.

"We'll meet you at the airport," Steph said.

"Yes, we'll meet you," Dave said.

Griff rolled his eyes. "Plane leaves at noon out of Eastman."

"We'll be there," Steph said.

Dave smiled widely at Griff.

Griff frowned, turned, and left.

Steph locked the door behind him. She turned to Dave. "Whose am I?" she asked with glee.

He was on her in a flash, his body pressing her against the wall. "You are my worst student ever." He held her gaze as he pulled back just enough to undo his jeans. She heard the rasp of the zipper and went damp. "I have to keep teaching you the same lesson over and over."

And then he lifted her and thrust inside.

"You're a good teacher," she gasped out as she wrapped her legs around him.

But her remark was lost in his constant chant of *mine, mine, mine* as he pounded into her.

The jet hummed as it soared through the sky. Steph squirmed as the three of them sat in awkward silence. She and Dave sat side by side on a white sofa on one side of the jet. Griff sat on an identical sofa across from them.

Griff scowled.

Dave smiled.

Dave's hand rested possessively on her upper thigh, occasionally stroking her, his fingers grazing scandalously high on her inner thigh. It was making her crazed, but she didn't protest. She needed Griff to get the message. They were done. Sign the damn papers.

Griff ground his teeth and finally broke the silence. "So… wanna drink? I've got a full bar."

Dave's fingers stroked inward, then up and down, up and down. She felt herself flush.

"We're good," Dave said, answering for both of them. "But thanks."

Griff stood abruptly. He returned a moment later with what looked like whiskey.

"Play a lot of concerts?" Dave asked.

"Tons," Griff replied flatly.

Another awkward silence fell. Dave stroked her leg again, sliding inward, up and down, up and down. Griff finished the whiskey in one long swallow.

"How's your opener?" Steph asked.

"They're good," Griff said. His eyes lingered on Dave's hand, which now gripped her inner thigh.

Dave's other hand was hidden from view, but it was sliding down her ass and then cupping her from underneath. Given half the chance, he'd lift her and drop her into a straddle right on top of him. She knew because he'd done that move plenty of times in exactly this position, one hand on her inner thigh, one on her ass. She figured it was no coincidence he was holding her like this. He was reminding her.

She tried to keep her breathing steady as she casually leaned back on Dave's arm to make him stop the wicked things his hand was doing, as his fingers now pressed on her insistently from underneath. He didn't take the hint.

"I picked the opener myself," Griff said. "Soul Cavity. They're like punk on speed."

Dave smiled, more like a baring of teeth. "Tell him about your tattoo, honey. It says Dave's. Right across her—"

"Dave!" Steph exclaimed.

"Oh, yeah?" Griff took off his leather jacket and rolled up the sleeve of his black T-shirt. He thrust his bicep forward. "See what that says."

Dave squinted at the Steph tattoo. "It says I'm a chump."

Griff leaped up. So did Dave. Steph jumped between them. "You guys promised me no fighting!" She glared at Dave. "You promised."

Dave sat down. Griff reluctantly sat down again.

"Now nobody is getting tattoos of any kind," she said in her best teacher voice. "No more fighting." She narrowed her eyes and took them both in with one icy glare. "Do I make myself clear?"

"Crystal," Griff said. He went back to the bar at the back of the jet to get another drink.

Dave palmed her ass. "Mine," he said fiercely.

She whirled around. "Dave," she whispered, torn between turned-on and exasperated. "Not now."

He pulled her down onto his lap and kissed her hot and deep until all her exasperation with him fled. He pushed her hair out of the way and nibbled along her neck. Griff rushed past them on his way to the front of the jet, where four chairs centered around a small table. He slammed his drink down on the table and flopped down into a seat, giving them his back.

"I think he's mad," Dave said with a devious smile before he resumed nuzzling her neck.

Steph sighed, tilting her head to give him better access. "I don't want him mad," she whispered. "I just want him to sign the papers. Don't antagonize him."

Dave pulled back. "He antagonized me."

"I don't care who started it..." She stopped herself. "This is ridiculous. You have to stop. Just enjoy the concert, we'll get the papers, and go."

"The only way I'll enjoy this concert is if you're dancing naked in it," Dave proclaimed.

"Shut. Up," Griff barked.

Steph giggled. Then she kissed Dave again to keep him quiet.

Dave cuddled up with Steph on the jet and pondered the past two weeks. He was still trying to wrap his head around the fact that he, Dave Olsen, middle school math teacher and upstanding citizen, had done the following: committed adultery (in a roundabout way), flaunted his claim in front of the husband, then got on the husband's jet to watch his concert. Once he'd met Griffin, he knew he had to come between Steph and her husband. That cheating jerk wasn't worth one picosecond of Steph's time.

Not only that, he'd spent the night in jail, and Steph, for some reason, had been hot for him when he got out. He kissed the top of Steph's head and glanced at her leather-clad husband, who appeared to be sleeping in his fully reclined seat. How could Dave deny Steph what they both wanted out of consideration for that asshole?

They went straight from the jet to a limo that took them to the stadium where Twisted Star was playing. Their luggage was delivered to the hotel for them. He and Steph were shown to private box seats while Griffin went backstage to warm up. The rest of the band was already there. They had some time before the show, so he and Steph toured the stadium and had dinner brought up to the private box, which was reserved just for them. The front of the box was all window. He couldn't tell if there were other private boxes, they only had a view of the stage.

When the opening band started, they settled on a long leather sofa together. Not Dave's kind of music, he preferred a mellower sound, but he was happy just to be sitting next to Steph, instead of sitting home wondering what she was doing with Griffin. After the opener finished, the stage went dark while the crew set up for Twisted Star.

Dave linked his fingers with Steph, who was sipping a mojito. She climbed into his lap. "Drink?" she asked.

"No, thanks. I want to have my wits about me when Griffin tries to weasel out of signing the papers again."

She tapped his nose. "You worry too much. He wouldn't fly us all the way out here for nothing."

"I don't think he intended to fly *us* out here. He wanted you."

She kissed him. He pulled away only long enough to set her drink on a nearby table. He wanted her thinking only of him when Griffin went on stage. He knew some of Griffin's songs meant something to Steph. Some of them made her feel deeply, and he wanted her to remember she was his. He kissed her passionately, gripping her hair to hold her in place while he claimed her mouth. After he'd gotten her to the point where she was making those little needy noises in the back of her throat, always a good sign, he set her off his lap, stood, and locked the door.

"Dave, what are you doing?"

She didn't sound particularly worried, only curious, so he said nothing. He crossed to her, buried his hand in her hair, and waited, his mouth hovering over hers. Her lips parted.

"Mine," he growled just before he kissed her. Things got hot and heavy fast. He pulled her onto his lap again, straddling him. He left her shirt on, but quickly undid her bra so he could caress her breasts. He kissed her as long as he could while she rocked her hips mindlessly against him, until he couldn't wait anymore. He pulled her to stand and moved her to the side of the box, away from the window, kissing her more as he undid the button and zipper on her jeans.

"Dave, people can see," she protested weakly.

"Shhh." He coaxed her with deep kisses, and his hand down her panties. She was hot and wet. His erection pushed painfully against his jeans. It was dark in the stadium, and he didn't think anyone could see them where they stood. At least not from the waist down.

He quickly stripped off her jeans and panties, undid his jeans just enough to free himself, and sat down on a low ottoman. He pulled her and settled her on top of his lap. She let out a shaky moan as she took him in. He hissed out a breath. She was so tight. Then she started to move. It felt so good he was afraid he wasn't going to last. He wanted to last. He wanted her riding him when Griffin went on stage. All of her attention on him. He gripped her hips and slowed her down, and every time she sped up, he put a hand on her waist, tipped her back, and used his other hand to distract her with slow circles around pleasure central. She whimpered, she begged, but he didn't let up, and he didn't let her speed up. It was a delicious torture for both of them and very, very necessary.

The first notes rang out as Twisted Star took the stage with an approving round of applause from the audience. He stilled Steph and suckled her breast, drawing it deep into his mouth. He knew she loved that. He could probably make her come that way if he did it long enough. She moaned and moved restlessly. He clamped his hands on her hips.

"Why won't you let me move?" she protested. "I want to move."

He didn't answer, merely teased her nipple with his teeth, doing his best to distract her with his mouth.

"Please, I want to move," she begged.

He ignored that. He caressed both of her breasts, pinching and tugging on her nipples, making her demands to move grow increasingly weak, until he finally silenced her with a hard kiss. He thrust his tongue in and out so she could do nothing but moan. He was very good at distracting her. And teaching her. He moved to nibble along her earlobe as he grabbed her ass, palming it with both hands.

"Mine," he whispered in her ear.

"Yours," she said on a sigh.

Pleased, he loosened his grip on her ass, and she moved on her own, too fast for him to keep things going. He stilled her again, hands on her hips, grinding her down hard onto him.

"Dave," she moaned. "Please."

It was hot, he had to admit, to have Steph begging him, but he had to wait. He rocked his pelvis, appeasing her with shorter strokes and some hip swivels. The opening number was building, and the crowd was roaring, and he wanted her focused only on them. By the time the band moved to the third song, they were both slick with sweat, their bodies straining for more.

He tilted his pelvis up, thrusting deeper inside, and released his hold on her. She immediately began riding him hard and fast. The buildup over all that time felt incredible as they rushed toward what their bodies ached for. He gripped her ass, felt himself about to lose it. Then she was crying out his name, milking him with her release, and he let go with a hoarse groan, shuddering against her. She collapsed against him.

They held each other for a few moments, catching their breath. She raised her head and looked at him like he was some kind of sex god. Or just an amazing guy. It was a flattering, well-loved look, whatever it was.

He flashed a smile. "Nice concert."

"What concert?" she replied.

He wrapped his arms around her. "Exactly."

10

———

Steph felt a little giddy as she held Dave's hand on their way backstage. They were headed through a private hallway with a security guard. She couldn't believe they did it in the private box. Sure they'd been alone, but there was a window. Probably Dave wanted Griff to see, but she knew Griff wouldn't have been able to see that far from the stage. It was twisted, she knew, but she liked this new possessive side of Dave. It was so sexy the way he claimed her. She'd hoped that his hot kisses when they first started dating were proof that things would be hot between them. She was thrilled to be proven right.

She turned to Dave and smiled. He squeezed her hand. Just as they reached the door leading backstage, the security guard, a beefy man that could've been a linebacker, raised a hand. "Only her. You wait here."

"What? No." Steph stood her ground. "Tell Griff it's both of us. I'm not leaving Dave behind."

"That's the deal," the security guard said. "Just you."

Steph looked from the security guard to Dave.

"I told you he only wanted you," Dave said.

She stood there, unsure what to do. She didn't want to leave Dave behind. On the other hand, the entire purpose of this trip was to get those signed divorce papers. She wasn't leaving here without them. She made a snap decision. The divorce was the most important thing. She'd get the papers and meet Dave at the hotel.

"I'll call you when I'm done," she said.

Dave looked like she'd slapped him. "You're really going backstage alone with him?"

"What choice do I have? I want that divorce. I'll meet you back at the hotel, okay?"

"Don't you see?" Dave asked, his face flushed red with anger. "He's playing with us. He's forcing me out. He still wants you."

She gave him a quick kiss. "It doesn't matter what he wants. It'll be fine. I'll call you."

The security guard held open the door, and she went through.

"Don't go," Dave called after her.

She turned. "I'll call you."

The door slammed shut as Dave stood there scowling at her. She'd make it up to him later. She followed the guard down a long hallway to a dressing room. She walked in to find Griff standing there, shirtless, a towel draped over his neck. His hair was soaked with sweat. The lights on stage were hot, plus he got a workout dancing, running, and putting his all into the concert.

"Hey, gorgeous," he said.

"Where's Paulie D?" she asked, looking around. "Where's Henry and Jake?" They were his bandmates.

"I got a private dressing room since you were coming." He flopped down onto a sofa. "Paulie D will be here soon. Did you like the concert?"

She crossed her arms, irritated to be alone with him instead of signing the damn papers. "You did a nice job."

"Nice," he muttered. He grabbed a bottled water and chugged, watching her. "Why Dave?" he finally asked.

She let out a breath of frustration. "What does it matter?"

"I want to know. It's hard to let you go, sweetheart."

She rolled her eyes. He'd let her go five years ago. Was he feeling nostalgic? Lonely? In need of a wife? Wait a minute.

"Do you need a wife for some reason?" she asked.

He shook his head. "Fans like to think I'm single. Tabloids like to talk about my secret wife. Nothing's up, if that's what you're thinking." He rubbed his hair down with the towel. "It's just once I saw you again in person I remembered what we had. It was good once."

She grunted. This was not going how she'd hoped. "How long until Paulie D gets here?"

Griff shrugged. "He said after the concert. Soon, I guess. Let me grab a shower." He indicated a private bathroom in the dressing room.

"Might as well," Steph said.

After Griff went into the shower, he left the bathroom door open, the exhibitionist, and she could see him through the frosted glass. She averted her gaze and flopped down on the sofa to wait. She called Dave to tell him she'd be a little later, but it went straight to voicemail. Strange. She wondered if he'd turned it off on the jet and forgot to turn it on again.

A short while later, Griff appeared with a white towel wrapped around his waist. Rivulets of water ran down his muscular chest and abs. Steph focused on his face. He gave her a slow smile.

"So you never told me why you like Dave," he said.

"Would you please get dressed!" Steph exclaimed.

He crossed to her, stopping a breath away, and she took in his fresh clean scent. She gave him a little shove, trying to preserve her personal space, and he grabbed both her wrists, then brought them down to her sides like they were almost holding hands. They were nearly the same height, and he was much too close, with way too little clothes.

"Why Dave?" he asked again.

She focused on a point over his shoulder. "He's a nice guy. Decent, hardworking, sweet."

And he's everything you could never be. Dave was faithful, committed, a family man. The life Dave offered was one she'd always wanted.

"I'm sweet," he countered.

She snorted. "Yeah."

"Look at me," he urged. Reluctantly, she met his eyes. "Isn't there some part of you that still loves me?" he asked quietly.

She pressed her lips in a flat line. "I'll never forget what you did, what you do, for Joey."

"He's a good guy."

Her heart squeezed. Not everyone saw just how wonderful her brother really was. "He always adored you."

"But what about you?" he asked. His hands, which had been gripping her wrists, now stroked the sensitive underside. "Do you have any love for me? I can work with the tiniest scrap if you just say the word. I can change. I'll be faith—"

"Don't." She pulled her hands away.

"Please, Steph. Don't make me beg."

"I don't love you." She forced the lie out because the truth was she'd always have a place in her heart for him. She wouldn't have married him if she hadn't loved him deeply. But that didn't mean they should be together. She'd moved on out of self-preservation. She wasn't indifferent to him, as much as she wished she was, though she could be once he left her alone again. And he would; she knew that. He wasn't the kind to stick around in one place for long. "I—"

Just then the door swung open, and Paulie D came in. Griff stepped away from her. Steph smiled at Paulie D, relieved they'd finally get this over with. Paulie D was a short man with balding hair and long, straggly pieces hanging down the sides. He was also a bundle of energy.

"Traffic was a bitch!" Paulie D exclaimed. He thumped Griff on the back. "How ya doin', Griff?" He turned to her. "Stephanie, we need to talk."

Talk? She thought she just needed to sign some papers. She glanced at Griffin, who turned away.

"Griffin can't sign the papers," Paulie D said. "This will destroy him. He's not exactly cash rich, if you know what I mean." He rubbed his fingers together. "The cash runs out just as soon as it comes in. It's the lifestyle—the mansion, the ski chalet, the island house. The jet. That's a shared ownership, by the way, with some other bands."

Griff quietly dressed in a T-shirt and jeans. He still wasn't saying anything. Steph was getting a bad feeling.

"I don't care about any of that," she countered.

Paulie D put his hands on his hips. "He's already behind on mortgage payments for the island house and, in this market, he's going to lose money on a sale for any of them. The high-end homes have taken the biggest hit depreciation-wise. I've advised him not to sell."

Steph huffed out a breath of frustration. "Aren't you listening to me? I just want the divorce. He can keep the money."

Paulie D cocked his head and narrowed his bulgy eyes. "Yeah, yeah, yeah. You say that now."

"I'll sign something that says that," Steph said.

"If only it were that easy." Paulie D started pacing. "Here's where it's complicated. If he signs those papers from Connecticut, they'll determine distribution of property in what they consider equitable. Connecticut won't rule favorably on account of his, uh, activities." His bulgy eyes shifted to Griff.

He meant all the affairs. She was so over that. Besides, she wouldn't demand half of everything. Unless…

She turned to Griff. "Either you give me the divorce right now, or I will get a lawyer and take half of everything. I've got a pretty good case against you. The infidelities are a matter of public record. You basically abandoned me."

Paulie D grew agitated, running his hands through what was left of his hair. "Now, hold on, hold on. No need for threats. We can work this out. If you could just hang on. A year from now we'll get the finances straightened out. You get a lawyer, and we'll settle this all up out of court. We'll make sure you've been compensated for your emotional distress. Maybe you could buy yourself a nice house in the suburbs. You'd like that, wouldn't you?"

"A year!" Steph exclaimed. "I've already waited five years. I don't want to wait a year." She snapped her head around to Griff, who was suspiciously quiet. "Griff?"

Griff shrugged one shoulder.

"Griff," she prompted, "are you going along with this?"

He sat on the sofa and pulled some socks on, then his black leather boots. Finally, he said, "It doesn't sound like a bad deal."

"I didn't come here for a deal!" she shouted.

"Give us a minute, Paulie D," Griff said.

Paulie D left, quietly shutting the door behind him.

"Why can't you just let me go?" she asked Griff.

He looked in her eyes. "Because I don't want to believe it's really over."

"Oh, you can believe it," she snapped.

Griff stood and crossed to her. "I'm sorry. It'll take some time, or whatever. When I get in a better position financially, maybe. Down the line. Things are going great. I've got a new album coming out in a few months. We're still putting the final touches on it. They love me in Japan. I'm planning a tour of Asia. Maybe I'll do a commercial over there too. Bill's in talks right now about it."

She sank to the sofa as the truth finally sank in. Dave had been right. Griff had played her. She should've expected it, yet she'd fallen for it because of their shared past, because of her brother, because of the seeming sincerity of his words. She felt stupid and angry and unbearably sad. This was all Griff could ever give, only the smallest gesture when it benefited him at the same time, and she'd wasted years of her life on him. He'd never had any intention of signing those divorce papers. And now she was supposed to wait another year? Suddenly, all she wanted was to see Dave again.

She shook her head as she pulled out her cell. "I can't believe this. I'm calling Dave." She called him, but it went to voicemail again. Dammit. Where was he?

Griff watched her. "Still not answering?"

She tucked her cell back in her purse. "No."

"Come on," Griff said. "I'll give you a ride back to the hotel. He's probably there."

She lifted her chin. "I can ride by myself in the limo."

"Let me go with you," Griff said. "I want to work this out. Let's talk about the divorce."

She eyed him suspiciously.

"No lawyers," he said. "Just you and me, working out a deal."

"I'm not—" But that was as far as she got before he pulled her forcibly out the door to the waiting limo.

Dave was not happy with the security guard escort out of the stadium and was even less happy when they got to a private parking lot, where a silver sedan with tinted windows stood waiting.

"Get in," the security guard said.

This was just like every thriller movie he'd ever watched. You should *never* get into the strange car with tinted windows. You could end up dead, or left for dead on the side of the road.

Dave backed up and found his way blocked by the guard's hand on his back.

The guard pushed him forward. "Get in. This is your ride."

"I'll call a cab," Dave said, pulling his cell from his pocket.

The man grabbed him by the arm and pushed him forward. Dave struggled; the cell hit the pavement and smashed into pieces. The front of the phone shattered. He could see the circuitry on the inside. Shit.

"You destroyed my cell!" Dave hollered before he ran. He didn't stop running until he was well clear of the stadium. Thankfully, the guard didn't follow him. He stepped into a convenience store, managed to get the clerk to allow him a phone call on the guy's cell, and called a cab back to the hotel. He could only hope that Steph would be waiting there with the signed papers.

Steph fumed on the limo ride back to the hotel. Griff tried to apologize for the legal complications, but Steph didn't want to hear it. He was like a puppet that just did whatever his people told him to. Even when that hurt the people he supposedly loved.

She looked out the window. It felt like they'd been driving a long time. She wasn't sure where the hotel was because they went straight from the airport to the stadium, but she'd thought when Griff's assistant reserved her a room, she would've picked somewhere close to the airport. "Where is this hotel?"

"West Hollywood," Griff replied. He glanced at her and quickly looked away.

"Is it much further?"

"I got us reservations for dinner. Reserved the whole place for late night. Cool?"

She gritted her teeth. "No, it's not cool. Dave is waiting for me. He thought I was just going backstage to sign the papers."

"Don't worry. He's at the hotel. Probably already asleep by now."

She scowled and called Dave again. Still went to voicemail. She was getting a very bad feeling about this. Why wasn't he answering his phone?

"Come on, Dave," she muttered, staring at her phone. It wasn't like him not to answer. Unless he was really, really mad at her.

The limo stopped. She peered out the window. They were stuck in traffic.

"Damn traffic," Griff said. "The one thing you can count on in L.A."

"What's the name of the hotel?" Steph asked. She'd try the room.

"Relax," Griff said. "I just want to be with you a little longer. You'll see Dave soon enough."

Panic shot through her. She reached for the door handle. "I'll walk back."

She tried to open it. Locked. She turned wide eyes to Griff.

"Chill, Steph. I'm not going to hurt you. I just want one last dinner. It's this cool place in Beverly Hills. You'll love it. We never did get to have dinner."

"Is the hotel the Sunset Marquis?" she asked, already looking up the number. It was Griff's favorite hotel. Rock stars loved the place because of its location, right off the Sunset Strip, near House of Blues, Roxy, and Viper Room, and it had a recording studio in the basement.

Griff smiled. "You remembered. Yup, that's the place."

She placed the call and asked for the room. The phone rang, twelve rings, no answer. She disconnected and stared at Griff. He held a crystal glass of whiskey in one hand, legs stretched out in front of him, mirrored aviator shades on as he gazed out the window. In that moment, he looked every bit the rock star he was, and she hated what he'd become. But she wasn't in a great position here. She just needed to get back to Dave. What must Dave be thinking right now? She went alone backstage with Griff and still hadn't come back hours later. He would think the worst. He usually did freak out where she and Griff were concerned.

"Did you take his cell?" Steph asked.

Griff frowned. "I'm not a thief. No."

"What did you do to him?"

He took a sip of whiskey, pushed his shades to the top of his head, and regarded her with annoyance. "I called for a car to take him back to the hotel. He's probably relaxing poolside at the Sunset. Poor guy."

She dialed again. Voicemail. She bit her lip. At least the limo was moving again. They'd exited the freeway and were speeding down some local road.

"I'll set up a trust for Joey," Griff said.

That got her attention.

"If you can wait one more year for the divorce," he said, "I'll make sure he's taken care of for life."

She felt like jumping at the offer. Lifelong care for Joey

would be a huge relief. Then again, Griff had used her brother as leverage before.

Steph heaved a sigh. "I feel like you're playing me again. Why should I trust that you'll do what you say?"

"You know I love Joey."

"That doesn't mean you'll keep your end of the deal."

"I really want to. A year from now I can have the money lined up. It's a win-win. You'll be happy. My people will be happy."

"You'll be happy you're not bankrupt."

He inclined his head.

"I don't know."

"Think it over at dinner."

She crossed her arms. "Dinner won't change anything between us. I'm sorry. That's just the way it is."

He blew out a breath. Then he surprised her by knocking on the window separating them from the driver. It rolled down.

"Take Steph back to the hotel," Griff said.

"You need better press," a feminine voice responded.

"Mandy?" Griff asked, clearly surprised. "Uh, I don't know what you think you're doing..." He trailed off. "Where's Rex?"

"Don't worry about him," Mandy replied. "Let's get you some good press."

"Forget it," Griff said. "Just take us back to the hotel."

An ominous click sounded and a gun appeared, wavering between her and Griff. Steph's heart stopped and then lurched forward.

"Mandy, calm down," Griff said gently.

"No one loves you more than I do," Mandy said.

The gun pointed at Steph. It was shaking as they were still speeding down the street. Omigod, Steph was gonna die in the back of a limo with the one man she'd hoped never to see again. This would be the last thing she saw—Griff, the limo, the white bench seat, psycho Mandy's gun. There would be no family left for Joey. Her marriage really would be until death do us part.

"Call Dave and tell him you're not feeling well," Mandy said.

Steph pulled out her cell and made the call, knowing it would go to voicemail.

"Put the gun away," Griff said. "We're all friends here."

The gun wavered between them. "You think I won't shoot you, Griff?" Mandy asked. "If you die young, you're a rock legend. I'd be doing you a favor. Like Elvis."

"Now, sugar, you know I could never be like Elvis," Griff returned smoothly. "He was the King."

"Then I'll shoot her," Mandy said with a laugh. "Then you'll be free."

"I'm already free, sweetheart," Griff said. "Let's make this a real pretty picture with me and Steph at the restaurant. We could be smiling or fighting, your call. But you'll get the exclusive."

The gun disappeared from view, and the window rolled back up. Steph's hands shook so badly she dropped her phone.

Griff pulled her into his arms and held her tight. "I'll get the gun as soon as we park," he whispered. "I won't let you die."

She nodded, her teeth chattering. Griff tucked her head under his chin, his arms protectively around her, and she clung to him, wishing she'd stayed home. She couldn't stop shaking. She knew Griff wouldn't want the cops involved. That would be bad publicity after his stint in jail, but she didn't care. This was life or death. What if Griff didn't get the gun before Mandy shot him? How far would Mandy go? Would she shoot them both and take off? Maybe she'd just shoot Steph if she wanted Griff to herself.

She untangled herself from Griff's embrace. If she was going to die, it wouldn't be in his arms. She picked up her phone and held it hidden in her hand.

"Where are we going?" she asked.

"It's this new place," he said. "The Poppy. Sounds pretty good now, huh?"

Yes, eating dinner with my idiot husband sounds lots better than getting killed by a psycho.

She nodded and looked out the window, biding her time. She wanted Griff's attention off her. When she felt enough time had passed that he wasn't completely focused on her anymore, she pressed her cell, intent on dialing 911, when Griff's hand shot out and closed over hers. They had a brief battle over the cell, but he was stronger and wrenched it out of her grasp.

"No cops," he said, tucking the cell into his back pocket.

She glared at him. "If I die, I will never forgive you."

He snorted. "If you die, I will never forgive myself. But calling the cops is just going to make her unstable."

"She's already unstable," Steph hissed.

"I can handle her."

She lunged for the cell, but he wrestled her away, pinning her flat on her back on the bench seat, her arms pinned at her sides. She struggled to no effect. "If we get through this, I seriously want to kill you."

He gave her his innocent choirboy face. "How is this my fault?"

"You're the one that lured me backstage, got rid of my boyfriend, got me into the limo—"

"Didn't you ever hear you shouldn't take candy from strangers?"

"This isn't funny."

"Do you trust me?"

"Hmm, let me think. No!"

"Steph, you know when the shit goes down I come through. Wasn't I there for you and Joey when your mother died?"

She blinked back tears at the reminder, but said nothing. He released her arms, and she sat back up.

"I promise I'll get you out of this safe and sound," he said. "I'm bigger and stronger than her."

"And she's got the gun."

"She won't use it."

"Oh, really. And how do you know this? Did the psycho

clear this with you first?" She jolted upright. "Omigod. Did you plan this whole thing?"

"Steph!" he chided.

"What?"

"How can you say that? I'm not a complete asshole. I would never scare you into publicity." He cradled her face with one hand as he always did when he spoke from the heart. "I promise you that."

She believed him. She pulled away from him. "She's still dangerous."

He shrugged. "She won't hurt me because she loves me."

"That's good for you," Steph said. "But what about me?"

"Do you love me too?"

She groaned. "Why do I even talk to you?"

He grinned. "Because you love me too."

She put her hand up in a stop sign. He grabbed her hand and pressed a kiss to the palm. She did not want to spend her last minutes on earth fighting with Griff.

"I hope you don't die," she said.

"That's the sweetest thing you've said to me in a long time," he replied. "Right up there with, oh, Griff, I'm coming!"

She shook her head. "I don't know how you can be so calm. I'm terrified."

He gazed warmly into her eyes. "If I had to be with anyone before death, I'd want it to be you."

Her throat felt tight. This was exactly why she'd fallen head over heels for him in the first place. The way he could reach out with such heartfelt emotion. It was what made his music so powerful.

"Oh, Griff," she managed over the lump in her throat. She really didn't want to die. She had so much she wanted to do in life. So much she wanted to share with Dave.

The car slowed to a stop.

Griff took a deep breath. "I love you, Steph. Never forget that."

Then he got out of the car to face Mandy. Why did he have to say things like that? She felt like they were his last words before facing a firing squad. He did love her, in his own selfish way. She heard Mandy yell, and Steph quickly ducked down on the seat.

Mandy yelled some more while Griff spoke in low tones. Mandy's voice lowered. Then things went eerily quiet. Her heart pounded. She might not want to stay married to Griff, but she certainly didn't want him dead. There was a scuffle, a woman's voice cried out, and a clanking of metal on metal.

All was quiet again. Sweat ran down her back. Did Mandy still have the gun?

The door opened, and Steph scurried back from it. Griff stuck his head in. "All clear. Get out here, beautiful."

"Is Mandy there?"

"She took off. Literally. She ran like a frightened deer."

Steph got out of the limo. They were in front of the restaurant Griff had reserved for dinner in Beverly Hills.

Griff ran his hands through his hair. "Still can't get used to not having the hair."

"Where's the gun?" she asked.

"I tossed it in that sewer grate," Griff said.

"What the hell, Griff!" Steph hollered.

He wrapped his arms around her. "It's okay. You're okay."

"What if she comes back?"

"She's a reporter for *Stars Chronicle*," he said. "She just wanted pictures and a good story."

Steph pulled away. "So she tries to kill us? Is she going to pull a gun on other celebrities for a story too?"

"I don't think she really wanted to kill us." Griff shrugged. "I think she just wanted to get pictures of us together on a date. That gun probably wasn't even real."

"It sure as hell looked real!" Steph paced back and forth on the sidewalk. "That was insane. You know that was insane."

"That's show business. Press can make or break your career. She was trying to help me."

Steph had no idea what to say. She was shaking again, thinking about how she almost died so that psycho could get a story. Where was Mandy? Was she going to show up at the hotel?

Griff pulled her close. "It's okay. She's harmless."

"Harmless?" Steph asked incredulously. "How can you be so casual about it? She pulled a gun on us!"

She extricated herself from his embrace and looked around. People were milling around, walking the sidewalks of Beverly Hills. Was there someone hiding in the bushes getting pictures of her with Griff's arms around her?

"Should we get dinner?" he asked.

She slammed her hands into his chest. "No! How can you be so calm?"

He held her hands, keeping them on his chest. "Crazy shit happens to me all the time. It goes with the territory. You can't have the fame without the crazies. Someone once sent me the dried-up umbilical cord from the baby son they named after me." At her aggravated look, he added, "It wasn't my son."

She yanked her hands free. "I'm calling a cab."

"Hold up. I'll drive you back." He gestured to the limo. "We've got wheels."

She let out a shaky breath. "I fucking hate you."

He tilted his head to the side. "Steph, you do not."

"I do. My life has been nothing but a roller coaster of one disaster after another since you showed up."

He reached out to her, and she jerked back. He dropped his hand. "You don't mean that."

She felt like crying as the adrenaline drained from her system, leaving her shaky and exhausted. Her shoulders slumped. This was the inevitable consequence of being drawn in by Griff. Everything went to shit. Never again, she vowed.

He took her hand and tugged. "Come on. I'll take you back to the hotel. Promise."

She went on shaky legs, unable to deal with any further hassle. "Fine," she snapped. "Let's go."

She slid into the front passenger seat. She left a message at the front desk for Dave. What she wouldn't give to have the strong, steady Dave at her side right now, instead of the laid-back, whatever-happens-is-cool Griff.

A cheerful Griff caught her up on his life on the drive to the hotel. She knew he was trying to put her at ease again after their scare. He told her of life on the road, all the cities, all the fans, the music. He still loved the music. She would've liked to tune him out, but she was so exhausted and drained that she could do nothing but close her eyes and let the words roll over her.

Griff pulled up to the hotel and squeezed her hand. "I'm sorry about all the craziness. I hope we can be friends."

"Sure," she said. "As long as I never have to see you again. Very long-distance friends. Like before."

He inclined his head with a small smile. "I can promise you with absolute certainty from someone that just looked death in the face that I will get the money together and, a year from now, that trust will be set up for Joey. Your brother will be set for life. Just give me one year, Steph. I *will* make it happen."

She simply had no fight left in her. And it was all for Joey. If any good could come from this whole ordeal, it was that. "Okay, Griff. Make it happen."

She got out of the car. It was late. Dave had probably gone to bed. She'd slip into the room quietly, and tomorrow they'd return home together.

The cab got stuck in a ton of traffic, but Dave finally made it back to the hotel. The first thing he did was call his sister from the hotel room phone. He needed someone to talk him down from this horrendous situation he'd found himself in because what he really wanted to do was kick Griffin Huntley's ass and scream at Steph for deserting him. Neither of which would win him any points with Steph. He told Christina the whole sorry tale. Of course she focused on completely the wrong part.

"You actually rode on his private jet?" Christina asked. "How was it?"

"It was lovely," he said in a voice dripping with sarcasm. "We enjoyed the finest wine and chatted about current events. What do you think!"

Christina let out a long breath that came through the phone loud and clear. "Why'd you go in the first place? He says jump, and you both say 'how high?'"

"Because Steph was going, and there was no way I was leaving her alone with him."

"But she's alone with him anyway."

"I'm aware of that," he said through clenched teeth. "I seriously want to rip his head off."

"Monster Dave," she muttered, then, "Oh, boy."

"What?"

"I just Googled Griffin Huntley. There's a picture of him and Steph in front of a restaurant. He's got his arms around her, and she kinda looks like she's hugging him back."

"Why do you keep telling me this shit?" He paced back and forth. "You know it makes me nuts. Do you want to see me go to jail for homicide?"

"It's probably an old picture," she said.

"We just went to the concert."

"How long ago?"

He glanced at the clock. *Time flies when you're in a panicky state in L.A. traffic.* "Two hours."

"Ah. Nope. Sorry. This is from today."

Why would Steph go to dinner with Griffin? She knew Dave was waiting for her. She was supposed to sign the papers and meet him at the hotel. Of course, then Griffin had one of his thugs send him away. And his stupid cell phone broke. Still, she could've called the room. There were no messages. He was done playing this game with Griffin and Steph. It was humiliating, and he always ended up with the short end of the stick.

"Chris?"

"Yeah?"

"Book me a flight home, would ya?" He pulled out his

credit card and rattled off the number. He'd be paying it off for the next couple of months with the ridiculous last-minute price he'd have to pay, but he didn't care. "I'm heading to the airport."

"All right. Sorry about this. I'll see you soon."

He hung up, got a cab to the airport, and got the last seat on a flight home.

11

Steph wasn't too surprised that Griff followed her into the hotel. The paparazzi liked to hang around the Sunset Marquis for celebrity sightings. Griff would never pass up the opportunity to be in the spotlight. She was exhausted. All she wanted to do was slip into bed with Dave and forget tonight ever happened. Some paparazzi took their pictures as Griff walked her to the front door, his hand on the small of her back. She hurried ahead of him.

He went inside, stopped, and kissed her on the cheek. "Bye, Steph. I'll be in touch."

She walked off to the front desk without a word.

"You too! Take care!" he called cheerfully. Always a performance. She ignored him.

A short while later, she headed to her room. Her luggage should already be there. The room was dark. She went in quietly. It was a suite with a separate bedroom from the living room area. She peeked her head in the bedroom. The bed was still made.

Panic licked through her. "Dave?"

No answer. This was not good. She turned on the lights and looked around for signs of him. She peeked in the bathroom, no Dave, no toiletries. She peeked in the closet. One suitcase. Hers.

She tried his cell again. No answer.

Had Dave left because she was late getting back? Was he that furious that she'd gone backstage without him? Didn't he get the message from the front desk?

She called his house and left a message. "Dave, it's Steph. I'm at the hotel. Where are you? I'm taking the jet back home tomorrow." She quickly decided not to mention the divorce papers still being on hold. That was a conversation they needed to have in person. "I hope to see you then. Bye."

She got ready for bed and checked her cell one more time for messages. There was a text from Griff: *Lay low for a while. Just a few pictures of us. No worries.*

She did a quick Internet search and found pictures of them embracing in front of the restaurant. Dammit! Was Mandy just hiding out to get those pictures? Had Griff pulled another publicity stunt? Oh, sure, he'd sworn he had nothing to do with it, but he'd also sworn in front of a minister that he'd be faithful to her for all of his livelong days. She seriously wanted to kill him. She'd been terrified. She didn't know if he was lying or not about Mandy. She clicked on another link. There was a picture of them walking into the hotel. A shot of when he kissed her cheek goodbye. How did these pictures get on the Internet so fast? They looked like a couple in the pictures. If this had been Griff's plan, she'd walked right into it. She never wanted to see him again.

She texted him back: *Go to hell.*

She turned off her cell and climbed into bed. Had Dave seen those pictures? Was that why he left? If only he'd answered his cell. Exhausted, she fell asleep determined to straighten everything out in the morning.

Steph got up early the next morning, turned on the TV, saw her picture on the news, and quickly turned it off. Shit. Dave was not going to like this one bit. She hated it too. She quickly got ready and called the number Griff had given her for her ride. She tried Dave's cell and his home number, but he wasn't answering.

She rode the jet home because she didn't want to deal with the hassle of finding her own way back. Besides, she had to

get to Dave as quickly as possible. She had to explain everything. It felt so strange to fly with just one person on the
plane. So different from their plane ride out to L.A. She only
hoped Dave was waiting for her back home.

Dave returned to his townhouse early the next morning after
the flight from hell. He hadn't slept at all on the plane as he
was both freaked out and squished into a seat without
enough leg room for a six-foot-two guy. Not to mention the
toddler in the seat next to him, who cried most of the flight.

He belatedly realized when he got home that he could
check his cell voicemail remotely. He listened as Steph's
messages grew increasingly worried, until the last message
that said she wasn't feeling well. His gut churned. What
happened to her with Griffin? Had he kidnapped her? That
last message had sounded not at all like Steph—strained and
almost…scared. Shit. Was she okay?

Dammit. He shouldn't have left L.A. without her. His
temper got the best of him. And, if he was honest, his pride. It
just felt like she always chose Griffin over him. But these
messages were scaring the crap out of him. Maybe Griffin had
done something to her. He never should've left Steph alone
with him.

He checked his voicemail at home and heard her message
that she was on her way back. At least she was well enough
to fly home. He called her, but it went to voicemail. Hopefully
she was on the plane. There was nothing to do but wait. He
tried and failed to sleep while he waited. He tried calling
Steph a few more times. His sister called for the latest news
and reassured him that things weren't as bad as they looked.
What the hell did she know? But he kept his thoughts to
himself because he knew she meant well. He finally settled in
front of the TV to wait.

A short while later, a knock at the door had him leaping to
answer it.

He opened the door. Steph stood there, suitcase at her

side. She looked exhausted, but she was all in one piece and had gone straight to him. His heart soared. "Steph."

"Dave!" She threw herself in his arms. It felt so good to have her there again he nearly forgave everything.

"What happened to you?" they said at the same time.

"You first," Dave said. "Are you feeling okay? What happened when you went backstage and after that?" His voice rose in fresh aggravation, even though he told himself the most important thing was that she was okay. His jealous, possessive side reared its ugly head. "I saw pictures of you at a restaurant, at the hotel—"

"Take a seat," she said. "I'll tell you everything."

They sat on the sofa. She took his hand, which felt like maybe she was trying to comfort him for bad news. He couldn't help but tense up.

"Steph, if you want to be with Griffin, just say so. I can handle it." He grimaced. "No, I can't. Just say it. No, don't." He jammed both hands in his hair. "What the hell is going on? Please tell me you're not with him. Did he kidnap you?"

"Would you just listen?" she asked. "The limo driver was this psycho reporter who pulled a gun on us."

"What!" He crushed her to him. "Omigod. Steph." He pulled back and cradled her face in both hands. "Are you okay?"

She blinked rapidly, her eyes shiny with tears. "Yes. Griff got the gun away from her and tossed it in the sewer."

"Where were you when all this happened?"

"Hiding in the back of the limo."

He crushed her to him again. She tugged on his arms, and he realized he was holding her too tight. He loosened his grip, but still kept her in his arms.

"Where's the psycho reporter now?" Dave asked. "Did you call the police?"

"She took off. Griff said she's harmless."

Dave stiffened. "Like hell she's harmless. She pulled a gun on you. And now she's just running free? What if she comes after you again?"

She let out a shaky breath. "I don't know. I didn't get a

good look at her either. Just the side of her face in the limo briefly before the gun appeared."

He crushed her to him again. "Dear God."

She hugged him back. "Griff wouldn't let me call the cops, but I will now. I don't even know her last name, but I know where she works."

"Good," he muttered. "That's good."

They stayed like that for a few minutes just holding each other. Finally, she sat up again. "I know those pictures looked bad, but they were completely innocent. I was freaked out about the gun, and Griff held me to calm me down. Then he gave me a ride back to the hotel. That's all that happened. I tried to get in touch with you, but your cell went to voicemail, and the hotel phone just kept ringing. I left you a message at the hotel."

"My cell broke," he said. "I got in a fight with a security guard."

"You got in a fight?" she exclaimed.

"He wanted me to get in this car, and I know better than to get in a strange—"

"Griff said he arranged for the car."

"Oh. Well, he might have let me know about that. Geez. I thought I was being knocked up."

She looked like she was trying not to laugh. "You mean knocked off?"

"Yes," he said fervently. "What's so funny?"

She clamped her lips together. "Nothing."

He gave her another suspicious look, and she kissed him. He wrapped his arms around her and kissed her with all the love in his heart. Still, some of the pieces weren't falling into place in his head.

He pulled away. "I was at the hotel, but they didn't give me a message."

"I swear I left one." She looked him in the eye. "The truth is, I think Griff wanted pictures of us to get out. He might have even been in on the whole gun thing. He acted strangely casual about it."

"He used you. Bastard. I'll kill him."

"So you believe me?"

"Of course I believe you. I should've known it was all him. Right from the start, he's been a total sleazeball."

She kissed him again. He buried his hands in her hair and kissed her breathless. Then he kept kissing her as he slowly pushed her back on the sofa until he was on top of her, between her legs, wishing there were no clothes between them. He pulled back just enough to look into her eyes. There was just one more thing he had to know. "Did you get the signed papers?"

Her eyes shifted to the side, and she turned her face away from him. "Not exactly."

He held her chin and turned her back to him. "Tell me *exactly* what happened. Did he weasel out of it again?"

She met his eyes. "Things are complicated financially for Griff. He said in a year a divorce would be easier."

He released her chin. "Fuck," he muttered. Fucking Griff, still fucking with them. He got off her. "A year. A whole fucking year. That's what he got out of you."

She stroked his arm. "Could you wait that long for me?"

He sat on the sofa, leaned forward and rested his elbows on his legs. "I don't understand. If you don't want his money, what's the difference? How the hell did he get another year out of you?"

She slid her arm around him, but he didn't want it there. That whole year thing was like a bucket of ice water splashed in his face. He straightened and slid away from her. She dropped her arm.

"He wants to settle out of court once he's stabilized his finances." She looked up at him with pleading eyes. "I know it's hard to understand, but I went along with it because Griff promised to take care of Joey. He's setting up a trust for him. He'll be taken care of for life. Griff thinks of him as family."

Dave shook his head. He was done playing by Griffin's rules. The man used her and used her brother as a bargaining tool. Bastard. "We're getting you a lawyer. You can settle all of this out of court right now."

"Paulie D told him not to sign anything."

"Who the hell is Paulie D?"

"His lawyer."

He took both her hands in his, trying one last time to get Steph on his side. "Steph, Paulie D doesn't get to decide about your life. This affects both of us."

"I'm okay with it. Just as long as Joey is taken care of. Please understand. I can't afford Horizon Village. Joey would have to move in with me. He'd miss his housemates and all the activities they have there. And I would be a package deal. Anyone in a relationship with me would have to be with Joey too. He's not that easy to live with. He has tantrums when his routine changes."

"Why in the world would you believe Griffin would keep his word?" Dave asked.

"He faced down a gun for me," she said. "If you could've heard him…it puts things in perspective when you're looking death in the face. I know he'll do this. He really does love Joey."

"I thought you said he was in on the gun thing."

"I don't know that for sure. He really did sound sincere when he promised to take care of Joey."

Dave frowned. "There must be other alternatives." He ran his fingers through his short hair and pulled. "Other group homes. Or we could all live together."

"You'd do that?"

"Yes. I'd like to meet him first, but…Steph, I really can't deal with Griffin any more. I want him out of the picture."

She stroked his cheek. "But we can still be together. We just can't get married right away. That's all."

He clenched his jaw. "You're choosing him."

"No, I choose you. I won't even see Griff again. It'll all be done by the lawyers." She gestured away from them. "Down the road."

His earlier anger came flooding back. "Why did you go backstage with him?"

She stroked his arm. "I'm sorry. I had my eye on the prize, the divorce, and I should've just told him to go to hell."

"Damn right."

He shook his head. He didn't like that she'd gone with Griffin while he was waiting at the hotel, but it did sound like Griffin's fault. Asshole.

Still, he couldn't help adding, "You let him put his hands on you."

She moved to straddle his lap, running her fingers through his hair. He went instantly hard, which was probably her intention. Distract him from his anger. He had to admit it worked. He was doomed to want her all of his life. Even while she was tied to another man.

"I was scared, that's all," she said, her fingers still trailing through the hair at the nape of his neck. "That doesn't mean I still love him or that I want to be with him." She wrapped her arms around his neck and gazed into his eyes. "I want to be with you. I'm yours." She kissed him. Her warm lips, so soft, and her taste enticed him, made him want to give in to it. And he did for a long moment, losing himself in the kiss.

But then he did the most difficult thing he'd ever had to do in his life. He lifted her off his lap and set her away from him. "I'm sorry. I can't do this."

"Because of Griff."

He said nothing. No amount of talking between them would change the fact that Griffin still held sway over Steph, and Dave didn't want to be caught in the middle anymore. He looked away.

"He's out of my life," Steph said. "I swear."

He turned back. "Who knows when he'll show up again? Ready to fly you in his private jet. Offering you diamonds. The world. And what do I have to offer you? A townhouse in Eastman. Help grading your math homework. I understand very well where I stand." He looked at the floor. "I love you so much it makes me crazy, but I can't live like this, caught between you and Griffin."

"Dave, please." Her voice broke, which made his chest clutch. "I choose you."

He met her eyes, which were shiny with unshed tears. "You let him get away with murder. Until you stand up to him, we don't stand a chance."

She blinked rapidly. "I'm not good with confrontation! I'm sorry! I'm working on it."

"Work harder, Steph."

"I have to balance things with my responsibility for Joey. Not everything is black and white. There's a lot of gray out there."

He stood. He had to remain firm, or he'd forever be caught in the tangle of Steph and Griffin. Forever be jealous, possessive, insane with frustration. That wasn't him. He was a nice guy. At least he used to be. He'd lost nice once Griffin showed up. He wasn't convinced Steph wouldn't see Griffin again either. The man did whatever the hell he wanted. If Griffin wanted Steph, he'd go after her, even if that meant staking out her house. He'd done it before. And Steph had done nothing to stop it. This was fucked up right from the beginning.

"I wish things were different," he said over the lump in his throat. "Goodbye."

Her eyes welled up, and he had to turn away so he wouldn't join her in a massive cry-fest. He heard her footsteps slowly head to the door, the suitcase wheels rolling behind her, the quick open of the door. She paused, and then quietly shut the door behind her. He let out a breath. He'd done the right thing. He was almost sure of it.

He sank to the sofa and dropped his head in his hands in complete misery. Sometimes it really sucked to do the right thing.

Steph went straight to Amber's house with her misery. She found her friend painting in the detached garage she used as a studio in the backyard. The garage door was partially open, and music blared from inside.

She knocked and called to Amber ahead of time so she didn't startle her. Amber could get lost in a painting and not come up for hours.

"Hey, you!" Amber called, shutting off the music and pulling the door all the way open. "How did it go in L.A.?"

Steph made it all the way to Amber's side before she broke down. Amber wrapped her arms around her.

Finally Steph pulled away and took a shaky breath. Everything came tumbling out all at once. "It went terrible. Griff asked me for another year to divorce because his finances are a mess, and I agreed because he promised to take care of Joey, but Dave doesn't understand, and he said I chose Griff, but I didn't, and now Dave doesn't want to see me!" That last part came out on a wail. "And a psycho pulled a gun on me!"

"What?" Amber exclaimed.

Bare poked his head out the back door. "Everything okay out here?"

Amber waved him away. "I got this, Bare."

He nodded once and returned to the house.

Steph sniffled. "You're so lucky you married the right guy the first time."

Amber smiled. "I know it. So tell me about the psycho first."

Steph filled her in and then told her all about Griff and their deal for her brother.

Amber listened thoughtfully. "Okay. Now tell me exactly what Dave said when he said he didn't want to see you."

Steph went through every detail, working hard to keep her voice calm and steady so Amber could understand her.

"Okay, forget about Griff," Amber said with a wave of her hand. "We just have to convince Dave to still be with you. Just because you can't marry him *yet* doesn't mean you can't be together. I think he's just hurt. Male egos are so fragile, you know?"

"Yeah?"

"Oh, yeah." Amber gestured for Steph to follow her further into the garage to a couple of chairs nearby.

Steph sat next to her friend. "Is Bare's ego fragile?"

Amber laughed. "No. If anything, he's overly confident." She shook her head with a smile. "I'm just speaking in general and from personal experience before Bare. My dad couldn't stand my mom doing anything that didn't involve supporting his career. Once she made it as an artist, he put down the entire field. He'll tell anyone that listens that art is a waste of time. I'm telling you—fragile."

"So what do I do?"

"You have to prove you love Dave and not the A-hole."

"How?"

"What does he like?"

Steph thought hard. "He likes math. And, um, Shrek."

"Oh-kay. Anything else?"

Steph crinkled her nose. "The ukulele."

Amber cracked up. "So you'll…" She waited for Steph to fill in the blank.

Steph dropped her head in her hands. "I have no idea."

Amber rubbed Steph's back. "You want me to have Bare talk to him? Man to man? People are always telling him stuff. He's like the easiest person in the world to talk to."

Steph shook her head. "No, but thanks. I guess I'll just learn to play the ukulele."

Amber grinned. "Or try calculus."

Steph groaned. Amber patted her back. "Don't worry. You'll think of something."

Things got worse. The next week was a firestorm of media attention over Griffin Huntley's secret wife. She didn't know what had escalated the story, but it was a national sensation. Press followed her to and from work, snapping pictures and firing questions at her. She tried to ignore them with a terse "no comment," but the questions kept coming:

"Why have you been hiding?"

"How do you feel about his other women?"

"Are you getting back together?"

She was afraid to go anywhere. She went straight home after work and refused to answer her phone. It was just the press calling. All of this attention and the pictures floating around of her and Griff were not helping her case with Dave. She'd even had to sit down and explain herself to the principal. Apparently, a lot of parents were calling the school wanting to know if she'd be leaving soon to reunite with her famous husband.

Griff sent her yellow roses with a note: Hang in there. Love, Griff. She threw them out.

Still no word from Dave. She'd tried calling him. He'd told her very firmly that there was nothing more to say between them as long as Griff was in the picture. As the days went by, Steph went from distraught to irritated with Dave. What happened to the guy who fought for her? The guy who kicked Griff's ass and landed in jail. What happened to the possessive guy that claimed her body, declaring it mine, mine, mine?

Damn fragile male ego.

~

Jaz and Amber showed up at Steph's place at the end of that media-frenzy week from hell for an intervention of sorts.

Steph answered the buzzer and could hear Jaz telling off some reporters.

"You'd better back the hell off," Jaz hollered. "The story is in L.A., not here."

"Get in here," Steph said in the intercom, buzzing them in.

She opened the door to find Amber clutching a brown bag and Jaz looking pissed off.

"We're here to fix your life," Jaz declared.

Steph snorted. "It's not broken."

Amber started unpacking the brown bag. Wine, potato chips, a pint of Shane's Scoops double chocolate fudge, and something called a Bliss SatisfyHer, which was a curved, knobby, twitchy-looking vibrator. Also, as big as a ferret. Steph shuddered.

"Uh…" Steph said.

"That's from me," Jaz said, pointing to the Bliss Satisfy-Her. "You don't need a man. And you've juggled two men long enough. Set them free and get on with your life."

Amber bit her lip. Steph thought about asking if Jaz had her own Bliss SatisfyHer, but was afraid to know. This had to be a joke gift. Right? She exchanged a look with Amber, who looked like she was about to bust a gut trying not to laugh. But Jaz wasn't laughing, so Steph refrained from looking a gift ferret in the mouth.

"The guys are free," Steph said, carrying the Bliss SatisfyHer to her nightstand drawer so Loki didn't mistake it for a vibrating hairless ferret and try to hunt it. She returned to the living room to find Amber pouring the wine.

The three of them settled on her sofa in front of the snacks. Amber handed her the ice cream and a spoon.

"So, how are you handling all the press?" Jaz asked. "Amber says you're hiding out here."

"I'm just trying to lay low," Steph said. She shoved a spoonful of double chocolate fudge into her mouth and savored the rush of flavor.

"Can I be honest?" Jaz asked. Steph and Amber exchanged an amused look. Like Jaz needed any encouragement to say what was on her mind. "You're handling this all wrong. I've had some brushes with fame during some of our more popular Broadway show runs. You just gotta live your life and keep the press in their place. Don't let them determine where you go or what you do. You wanna go out for a drink at Garner's? You go. You want to walk your cat, you go."

Steph and Amber cracked up.

Jaz grinned. "For real, you know what I'm saying?"

"I know," Steph said.

"Have you heard from Dave?" Amber asked gently.

Steph took a long swallow of wine. "Dave won't talk to me until Griff's out of the picture."

"He is out of the picture," Jaz said. "He's in L.A. You're here."

"I know," Steph said miserably. "Dave's mad that I want to wait a year for the divorce. Griff said if I did, he'd set up a trust for Joey for the rest of his life. You guys know how much that means to me."

"He doesn't want to share you," Jaz said, pouring Steph more wine.

"Men are touchy that way," Amber chimed in.

"Tell me about it," Steph muttered.

"Why a year, though?" Jaz asked. "What's so"—she wiggled her fingers in the air—"magical about a year for a divorce?"

"His lawyer wants him to have time to get his finances in order," Steph said.

Jaz did her classic head roll. "His lawyer? Un-uh. No way." She took Steph's wine and ice cream away from her. "Stephanie Moore!" she hollered.

Steph jumped. Amber stared, mouth gaping.

"Repeat after me," Jaz barked. "We do not let lawyers run our lives."

"We do not let lawyers run our lives," Steph said hesitantly.

"Stand up," Jaz ordered, pulling Steph to her feet. "We do not let *the press* run our lives."

Steph stood with a glance at Amber, who was smiling into her wineglass.

"We do not let the press run our lives," Steph said, stronger now.

"We do not let men steal our happiness," Jaz barked.

Amber giggled. Jaz shot Amber a quelling look.

Steph stood up straighter. "We do not let—"

"Louder, girl!" Jaz commanded.

"We do not let men steal our happiness!" Steph yelled.

Jaz high-fived her. "That's what I'm talking about. You walk tall and proud. Fuck that lawyer, fuck the press, and fuck the men who fuck with your head."

"Amen," Amber said.

"Amen," Steph said solemnly as Jaz handed her wineglass and ice cream back to her.

They sat on the sofa again. Jaz raised her glass, and the three of them clinked glasses in a toast.

"To strong women," Jaz said.

"To strong women," Steph and Amber echoed.

"Fucking A," Jaz said.

They all drank to that.

"Now what's your plan for reclaiming your happiness?" Jaz asked. "It's yours for the taking."

"My new Bliss SatisfyHer?" Steph asked.

Amber cracked up. Jaz grinned. "That's a start. Don't really use that thing, by the way. That was a gag gift."

"Oh, yeah," Steph said. "I mean, I knew that."

Amber nodded vigorously. "Good one, Jaz."

One corner of Jaz's mouth lifted in a small smile. "Do you really want Dave back after he blew you off?"

Steph sighed. "I do. I still love him. I think if Griff wasn't part of the deal, we probably would be engaged by now."

"Seriously?" Amber asked.

Steph nodded. "He said he wanted me to have his babies."

Jaz choked on her wine. "He actually said that?" She turned to Amber, incredulous. "What guy says that?"

Amber shrugged. "A guy who wants a future wife and mother to his children."

Jaz blinked rapidly. "That is *so* damn sweet. Hell, yeah, we want Dave back." She turned to Steph. "What's your plan?"

Steph shrugged. "I don't know. Nothing's changed as far as Dave's concerned. I'm still married. I'm still tied to Griff."

"And?" Jaz prompted.

Steph took a deep breath. It was time to face confrontation head-on. She set her wine and ice cream on the table quite firmly. She stood and looked at her two friends, who she knew had her back.

"And I'm getting my own lawyer and ending this marriage," Steph announced.

Jaz cheered. Amber gave her a high five.

Steph went on, feeling more confident now. "And I'm going to use the press to turn this story around. This was Griffin's fault, and Dave and I shouldn't have to suffer."

Jaz and Amber clapped.

Steph smiled. "And I'm going to use Dave's little head to reach his big head."

"Woo-hoo!" Amber cheered. "Naked works."

Jaz nodded her approval. "Naked always works. And, if not..." She looked around. "Where is that thing? Gotta love a

Bliss SatisfyHer. I'll bet a man came up with that name. A woman would just call it what it was—The No-Man-Needed Pleasure Tool."

"That's not very catchy," Amber said. "I'd just call it Bliss Starter." She held up a hand. "No, Bliss Assistant."

"Hey, that's nice," Jaz said, lifting her glass of wine in a sex-toy-approved toast. Amber toasted back. "Classy. You may have a future in the sex-toy industry."

"Why, thank you," Amber said. She raised her voice to a singsong high pitch. "My *highly intellectual* physicist father would be so proud."

Steph piped up. "Ladies! Never mind the sex-toy industry. There's just one small problem, a lawyer is expensive."

"You know what?" Jaz said. "Start a Kickstarter campaign to raise the money. Ooo-hoo-hoo. Wouldn't that play out in the press? Schoolteacher raises funds to divorce her rich rock star husband."

"That could work, actually," Amber said.

"I could never ask other people to fund my divorce," Steph said. "It's my problem, not theirs."

Jaz stood and slung an arm over Steph's shoulders. "I just want to see you happy. Whatever you need to do, I'm here for you."

Amber slung an arm over Steph's shoulders from the other side. "Me too."

Steph blinked back tears. "You guys."

"All right, let's get drunk and watch a rerun of *Sex and the City*," Jaz declared. "I am way into Steve. Miranda doesn't appreciate his heart of gold."

Steph shook her head. "Steve's kind of geeky, isn't he?"

Jaz took a sip of wine and put a fist on her heart. "It's the heart, babe. All the way."

Amber raised her fist and gave Jaz a fist bump.

Steph settled in, cozy on the sofa, cushioned by her friends. She knew what her heart wanted. She just needed to wade through all the crazy to find a way back.

12

———

Dave couldn't go anywhere without someone feeling sorry for him. Steph and Griffin were all over the news, the Internet, the tabloids. His guy friends tried to console him with the classic, "there's other fish in the sea," but he knew there never would be. Steph was it for him. But he wasn't it for her.

His mind kept returning to the conditional statement:

IF Steph + Griffin THEN

end Steph + Dave

ELSE

Steph + Dave.

He'd never wanted a conditional statement to be false so much in his life. He wanted ELSE. But Steph had to come to him. She had to choose him and, more importantly, get rid of Griffin.

His women friends just gave him soft words and sympathetic looks. They knew how much this sucked for him. Courtney (French teacher) had even offered to kiss him in a selfie and post it online to make Steph jealous. He'd declined her kind, but misguided offer. She'd then whispered, privately away from the teachers' lounge, even more inappropriate things they could do, which just made him chuckle.

"Thanks, Courtney, I needed that," he said.

She tossed her hair and strode away. She was quite the jokester.

Chris kept bugging him to fight for Steph, but he was done fighting. He fought Griffin for as long as he could. He'd fought to claim Steph in the most primal way and still…he felt like he'd always have to share her. She'd always be torn between the two of them. This was exactly why polygamy was illegal. And especially rare with one woman and two men. Men did not share their woman easily.

Chris called him after work with another one of her "brilliant" ideas. He sighed heavily.

"No," he said, "but thanks for thinking of me."

"It would work," she insisted. "He hogs the press with your woman, then you fight back in the press. You hog the press. There's nothing Griffin Huntley loves more than publicity. Putting you in the spotlight would drive him nuts."

"First of all, no one cares about me—"

"Yes, they do!"

"And, second of all, I don't want publicity. I just want Steph with no Griffin in the picture."

"This is what I'm saying, doofus."

"Forget it."

"Don't make me do what's best for you."

"Chris, I swear—"

"You're welcome." She hung up.

She wouldn't really go through with it, he reassured himself. Not if she wanted to live through another family dinner. His parents would take his side on this one. Well, his dad would. He pushed that out of his mind. No one would pay any attention to Chris. No one cared about him enough to report on him. It was fine.

Steph showed up at Dave's door that night wearing her taupe belted coat with stilettos and nothing else.

He regarded her warily. "What are you doing here?"

She pushed past him and dropped the coat.

He swallowed visibly. She waited. A beat passed while they stared at each other. Then she said the one thing she knew would press his button.

"Game on, Dave. I dare you."

He shook his head slowly, and her heart stopped. Then he scooped her up and carried her toward the bedroom.

"You should never dare me," he said before he tossed her on the bed. "Game fucking on."

Steph reveled in it. After a lot more dares and a lot more loving, Steph snuggled into Dave's side and traced a circle over his chest. "I think I know how to convince Griff to move things along."

He pulled back to stare at her. "You do?"

"Yeah, though it might mean some press for us. Are you okay with that?"

He sighed heavily, muttering, "This again."

"What?"

"Nothing." He kissed her hair. "Okay, fine. I'll do anything to get him out of the picture."

She let out a breath. This could be embarrassing, especially if her students saw the press, but it was time she put her and Dave first.

Griffin did a double take when he got the email from his publicist. It was a photo of Steph and Dave, their arms wrapped around each other, as she looked up at him adoringly. But that wasn't what got to him. Steph was dressed as Fiona from *Shrek*, complete with ogre ears. Dave wore his ogre ears too.

His chest clutched. He'd lost his muse. His music would never be the same again. He poured a shot of whiskey and tossed it back. The Steph he knew would never dress like an ogre. The woman hated to even leave the house without lipstick. For her to let herself be photographed like this meant only one thing—she was really and truly in love. And though she'd told him that, he hadn't really believed her. He'd been caught in the memories of what they'd once had, and some part of him kept thinking he could get her back given enough time.

He called Paulie D. "I'm signing the papers."

"I don't advise—"

Griffin hung up. Next he called his accountant to arrange a few things. He had houses to sell, a trust to set up for Joey, cash to raise.

He sent the papers to Steph with overnight delivery. Then he did what any rock star would do. He drank whiskey, took a long shower, sank to the shower floor, and sobbed. It was really over. He'd lost his muse. He'd lost his music. He had nothing left.

Steph had no idea what that one picture of her and Dave would unleash. They went back to his place after work only to find a crowd of press waiting with cameras and microphones. All eager to hear from Dave.

"Little Genius, where've you been hiding all these years?"

"Are you going back into show business?"

"How did you stay out of the spotlight for so long?"

Dave's hand tightened on hers. He seemed frozen, staring at one camera that was trained on him.

"Dave?" she asked. "What's going on? What are they talking about?"

"No comment," Dave said to the press and pulled her inside the house.

He turned on the TV and went to his laptop. Steph stared incredulously as the news flashed Dave's school teacher picture next to a picture of Dave as a little kid. He was adorable, a miniature version of the man she knew, his brown hair parted neatly to the side, already wearing round glasses.

The reporter looked into the camera. "Little Genius, we've missed you. You must be a big genius now."

Dave groaned at the laptop. "It's everywhere. I thought it would just be you and me in the Shrek outfits."

He shut the laptop and turned off the TV. He sank to the sofa and dropped his head in his hands. "I'll kill her."

She sat next to him and put her arm around him. "Kill who?"

"Chris. I told her not to do anything."

"What did she do? Was that really you?"

He let out a heavy sigh and explained he was the kid who starred in a series of Little Genius commercials when he was four. Little Genius was a laptop for kids. She'd loved those commercials of the little boy who confidently answered all the tricky math questions thanks to his Little Genius laptop. He was so earnest in his answers, and he had a slight lisp. He also dropped some of his Rs in the kid version of a Brooklyn accent. It was all so freaking adorable.

"Chris said it would be good publicity for me," Dave said. "To shift the spotlight away from you and Griff, but I told her not to do it. Figures she wouldn't listen."

Steph still couldn't believe he was *the* Little Genius. "How did you get into show business?" she asked. "And so young."

He merely shrugged. "Mom took Chris and me on auditions in the city when we were little. She wanted us to earn money for college."

"Did you?"

"Yeah. Chris did too. She did a lot of modeling for kids clothes catalogs."

"I can't believe my boyfriend is famous. Here I thought you were just a regular guy."

He turned to her. "It's stupid, isn't it? That's why I never tell anyone." He mimicked his little kid voice. "Little Genius, more than just a calculataw." He shook his head. "They loved the way I mispronounced calculator."

She hugged him. "I loved Little Genius!"

One corner of his mouth lifted. "Yeah?"

"Yeah. And it's so hot that I get to be with Big Genius. What a sexy charmer."

He pulled her into his lap. "You just can't help but get tangled up with charmers, huh?"

"Only one charmer."

He kissed her long and deep, and started pulling her toward the bedroom.

"Wait," she said, breathless. "I've got something to show you."

He waggled his brows. "I've got something to show you too. Me first."

He snagged her around the waist, pulling her close for a kiss that was hard and demanding. Slow and gentle Dave seemed to have left permanently once Griffin arrived on the scene. He had one arm banded around her waist, holding her tight against him as his mouth claimed hers. She gave up on showing him her surprise, looping her arms around his neck and kissing him back passionately.

A noise out front reminded them they had company. Dave jerked back. He pressed his thumb to her lower lip with a heated gaze. "Give me one minute."

He turned and opened the front door. "Hey, all. I'm about to get lucky with the love of my life, so if you could come back tomorrow morning at eight a.m., I'd be happy to tell you all about Big Genius and his new way of calculating numbers using higher mathematics."

Camera flashes went off. Some of the reporters chuckled.

"Dave!" Steph exclaimed with a laugh.

Dave shut the door and locked it. He closed the blinds too. While he was watching out the small front door window for the reporters to leave, she went to her purse for the FedEx envelope she'd wanted to show him.

A few minutes later, he turned to her with a grin. "They're gone. For now, anyway."

She laughed and handed him the envelope. "Signed divorce papers."

He pulled out the papers and read them. He stared at the signature. Just kept staring.

"Aren't you happy?" she asked. "I thought you'd be jumping up and down."

He stared at her. "I think I'm in shock."

"Well, be happy!" She threw her arms around him.

He blinked. His eyes were shiny with unshed tears. "I've

never been happier." He set the papers on the coffee table and turned to her. "Steph, will you marry me?"

"Yes!"

He cradled her face with both hands. "Will you have all my Little Genius trademark babies?"

She laughed. "I would love to have all your Little Genius trademark babies."

He dropped his hands and whispered in her ear, "I've done research on a woman's erogenous zones."

A flash of heat went through her. "I can't wait."

Dave practically ripped off her clothes before tossing her on the bed. Good for his word, he worked through all her erogenous zones, telling her exactly what he planned on doing, waiting for her to say it was his, all his, before following through while she quivered from his thorough attention.

She didn't mind one bit when he woke her in the middle of the night. He couldn't see much in the dark without his glasses, so he said he'd have to go by touch and taste. He worked his way down her body, and just when she couldn't wait another second to have him inside her, he flipped her over and explored from the nape of her neck down to her toes. She had never felt so cherished, so well loved in her life.

At breakfast, he made her an omelet and fed her bits of it while he held her on his lap. She wore an oversize Columbia sweatshirt and nothing else, at his request. He'd bought an extra Columbia shirt for his place because he loved to see her in it. Apparently, brains were a real turn-on for him.

"I can't wait to make you all mine," he told her.

"I dare you."

Dave didn't need any more encouragement.

Griffin couldn't believe the firestorm of press over Dave. The man was a phenomenon. They called him Mr. Genius because of those commercials he'd done as a kid. It had been a month, and Dave had already done a geek-chic modeling job and a few commercials for some new electronic learning system. While Dave was moving up, Griff was scaling down. His focus was back on the music, not the lifestyle. It was first, last, and forever about the music. That was something Christina had reminded him of. As crazy as she was, she kept it real.

A thought hit him. Christina. She had to have been the one to leak out the news about Dave being in those kiddie commercials. Sure, with some digging the press could've found out about Dave's commercials, but the way the news spread so quickly after that Shrek picture, it had to have been her. Dave would've revealed that tidbit a lot earlier if he really wanted to snag the spotlight. Griff would've thought of Christina's devious role in all this sooner, except he was too busy selling off his properties and getting ready to move to a brownstone in Brooklyn. Paulie D had thrown fits about it. Griff had fired him. In fact, he'd let all of his staff go, except his manager, Bill. He'd also filed a restraining order against Mandy. He'd had stalker fans before, some weird shit women gifted him with, but never someone that pulled a gun on him. He'd been shaking in his boots when that happened, but he'd kept his cool for Steph's sake.

The music scene in Brooklyn was hopping. He couldn't wait to be part of it. And he could easily visit Joey from there. He pulled out his cell and texted Christina. He had her number programmed in his phone as Crazy Christina. He didn't know why he'd bothered to program it in. He'd never intended to call her. His text said simply: *I know it was you.*

She replied immediately: *Took you long enough, Sherlock.*

He smiled and texted back: *I'm moving to Brooklyn. I hope I never see you.*

She texted: *Your ugly mug belongs in Cleveland.*

He broke out into a wide grin and replied with a smiley face. She meant he belonged in the Rock and Roll Hall of Fame in Cleveland.

She texted back. *An emoticon? I expect more from a badass rocker. Fail.*

He replied with a shocked face emoticon.

Then she reached out through the power of text, grabbed

him by the collar, and sent a bit of poetry: *I want to hear your soul music. No matter how long it takes to get your shit together. Hear me?*

He sucked in a breath, touched by her faith in him. He replied: *You're a ballbuster.*

I'm your fucking muse.

He immediately heard the beginnings of a rip-roaring guitar riff.

Tell me what pisses you off, he texted.

She went on and on. Her words became the lyrics to a new song, "Crazy Thing." He'd found his muse. Crazy Christina opened up a very different vibe in him. It was euphoric.

EPILOGUE

"So how does it feel to be Mrs. Olsen?" Dave called from the bedroom. They were at his family's lake house for what promised to be a beautiful summer-long honeymoon. They'd be house shopping soon with the money from Dave's modeling gig and commercials.

Steph pulled the red satin and lace robe over the matching slip she'd picked out for their wedding night. She was dressing in the bathroom to surprise him. "It feels great!"

She smiled as she pulled her hair up, leaving a few tendrils to hang down. After her divorce was final, she and Dave had immediately planned a church wedding and reception for the weekend after the school year ended. Someone had made a huge anonymous donation to their school district's music program. Steph had a feeling she knew exactly who it was. The same benefactor that had established a trust in her brother's name. Griff had a new hit getting a lot of attention, inspired by, of all people, Dave's sister. She'd hit it off with Christina right away, both women passionate about family.

She grabbed her surprise for Dave, hid it behind her back, and stepped out of the bathroom. "How does it feel to be a married man?"

He took her in, head to toe, and swallowed visibly. "I've never been happier in my life."

"Good," she practically purred. She sauntered over to him where he lay on the bed wearing only his black Dr. Who boxers that read Trust Me I'm the Doctor. She kissed him and, while his eyes were closed, slipped on her surprise for him. She pulled back. "How do you feel about a little role-playing?"

She wore a Princess Fiona wedding headband—ogre ears with a small tiara and veil.

"I thought you'd never ask," Dave said fervently. "Be right back."

She sat up and watched as he rummaged through his suitcase and came up with his ogre ears and handcuffs. He shoved the ears on his head. "First you need to be rescued," he said, striding over and snapping the cuffs on her.

She wrapped her cuffed arms around his neck. "Yes, my adorable ogre."

He pushed her gently back on the bed, shifting the pillow so it was under her head. Slow and gentle Dave was back. Though she could still bring out the animal in him with a well-timed dare. He was very competitive and could never turn down a challenge. She liked to let him win by a landslide, leaving them both panting and satisfied.

He met her eyes with a grin. "Then I have to transform you into the human princess by working every erogenous zone I've researched!"

"Oh, Dave." She shivered, knowing how intent his focus and attention could be.

He leaned close, his lips just a breath away. "How do you feel about being Uhura tomorrow night?"

"Uhura?"

"From *Star Trek*?"

"I, uh, like it?"

He closed his eyes. "You haven't seen the original *Star Trek*, have you?"

"No." She bucked her hips to remind him what was

important. She could feel his erection pushing against her through the boxers.

"We'll stream it on the laptop," he croaked.

"I dare you to make me scream."

Dave got right to work. And he didn't stop until much, much later when she screamed his name like a freaking hallelujah.

What an alpha!

Don't miss the next book in the series, *Almost Fate,* featuring Griffin and Christina on their way to happy-ever-after. Or not.

Almost Fate

Rock star Griffin Huntley longs for the one thing he never had—family. And who better to give it to him than his girlfriend, manager, and muse, Christina Olsen. But when his New Year's Eve marriage proposal hits a sour note, Christina flees his limo in the middle of Manhattan, leaving Griffin fearing the worst.

Christina has been burned in marriage before and knows marrying Griffin would be the kiss of death in their relationship. Just look at the disaster with his first wife. But when Griffin is spotted in the press with not one but two beautiful women, Christina has a few choice words to say. To his face.

Only what she discovers is a secret from the past taking over Griffin's life. Can two people with scarred hearts ever leave their pasts behind or does fate have other plans?

Sign up for my newsletter and never miss a new release! https://www.kyliegilmore.com/newsletter

ALSO BY KYLIE GILMORE

Unleashed Romance <<steamy romcoms with dogs!

Fetching (Book 1)

Dashing (Book 2)

Sporting (Book 3)

Toying (Book 4)

Blazing (Book 5)

Chasing (Book 6)

Daring (Book 7)

Leading (Book 8)

Racing (Book 9)

Loving (Book 10)

The Clover Park Series <<brothers who put family first!

The Opposite of Wild (Book 1)

Daisy Does It All (Book 2)

Bad Taste in Men (Book 3)

Kissing Santa (Book 4)

Restless Harmony (Book 5)

Not My Romeo (Book 6)

Rev Me Up (Book 7)

An Ambitious Engagement (Book 8)

Clutch Player (Book 9)

A Tempting Friendship (Book 10)

Clover Park Bride: Nico and Lily's Wedding

A Valentine's Day Gift (Book 11)

Maggie Meets Her Match (Book 12)

The Clover Park Charmers series <<sweet and sexy charmers!

Almost Over It (Book 1)

Almost Married (Book 2)

Almost Fate (Book 3)

Almost in Love (Book 4)

Almost Romance (Book 5)

Almost Hitched (Book 6)

Happy Endings Book Club Series <<the Campbell family and a romance book club collide!

Hidden Hollywood (Book 1)

Inviting Trouble (Book 2)

So Revealing (Book 3)

Formal Arrangement (Book 4)

Bad Boy Done Wrong (Book 5)

Mess With Me (Book 6)

Resisting Fate (Book 7)

Chance of Romance (Book 8)

Wicked Flirt (Book 9)

An Inconvenient Plan (Book 10)

A Happy Endings Wedding (Book 11)

The Rourkes Series <<swoonworthy princes and kickass princesses!

Royal Catch (Book 1)

Royal Hottie (Book 2)

Royal Darling (Book 3)

Royal Charmer (Book 4)

Royal Player (Book 5)

Royal Shark (Book 6)

Rogue Prince (Book 7)

Rogue Gentleman (Book 8)

Rogue Rascal (Book 9)

Rogue Angel (Book 10)

Rogue Devil (Book 11)

Rogue Beast (Book 12)

Check out my website for the most up-to-date list of my books:
kyliegilmore.com/books

ABOUT THE AUTHOR

Kylie Gilmore is the *USA Today* bestselling author of over fifty humorous contemporary romances. Her series include Unleashed Romance, the Rourkes, the Happy Endings Book Club, Clover Park, and Clover Park Charmers. With more than three million downloads of her books, readers all over the world love escaping into her hilarious feel-good romances featuring strong bonds with family, friends, and community.

Kylie lives in New York with her family, a demanding cat, and a nutso dog. When she's not writing, reading hot romance, or dutifully taking notes at writing conferences, you can find her flexing her muscles all the way to the high cabinet for her secret chocolate stash.

Sign up for Kylie's Newsletter and get a FREE book! kyliegilmore.com/newsletter

For text alerts on Kylie's new releases, text KYLIE to the number (888) 707-3025. (US only)

For more fun stuff check out Kylie's website https://www.kyliegilmore.com.

Thanks for reading *Almost Married*. I hope you enjoyed it. Would you like to know about new releases? You can sign up for my new release email list at kyliegilmore.com/newsletter. I promise not to clog your inbox! Only new release info, sales, and some fun giveaways.

I love to hear from readers! You can find me at:
kyliegilmore.com
Facebook.com/KylieGilmoreToo
Twitter @KylieGilmoreToo

If you liked Dave and Steph's story, please leave a review on your favorite retailer's website or Goodreads. Thank you.